KING PENGUIN

LOVE

Angela Carter was born in 1940; she published her first
novel, *Shadow Dance,* in 1965 and was immediately recognized as one of Britain's most original and disturbing
writers. Since then, she has written seven other novels,
three collections of short stories, two books of nonfiction,
a translation of the fairy tales of Charles Perrault, and
numerous poems and pieces of journalism. She is the
author of the screenplay for *The Company of Wolves,* a
fantasy film; a collection of her radio scripts was published in England in 1985. Her *Saints and Strangers, The
Bloody Chamber, Fireworks,* and *Heroes and Villains* are
also available from Penguin. Carter lives in London but
frequently teaches in the United States, most recently at
the University of Texas and at the Iowa Writers'
Workshop.

LOVE

ANGELA CARTER

A KING PENGUIN
PUBLISHED BY PENGUIN BOOKS

PENGUIN BOOKS
Published by the Penguin Group
Viking Penguin Inc., 40 West 23rd Street,
New York, New York 10010, U.S.A.
Penguin Books Ltd, 27 Wrights Lane,
London W8 5TZ, England
Penguin Books Australia Ltd, Ringwood,
Victoria, Australia
Penguin Books Canada Ltd, 2801 John Street,
Markham, Ontario, Canada L3R 1B4
Penguin Books (N.Z.) Ltd, 182–190 Wairau Road,
Auckland 10, New Zealand

Penguin Books Ltd, Registered Offices:
Harmondsworth, Middlesex, England

First published in Great Britain by
Rupert Hart-Davis Ltd 1971
This revised edition published in Great Britain by
Chatto & Windus Ltd 1987
Published in Penguin Books 1988

10 9 8 7 6 5 4 3 2 1

LIBRARY OF CONGRESS CATALOGING IN PUBLICATION DATA
Carter, Angela, 1940–
    Love:a novel/Angela Carter.
    p.   cm.
    I. Title.
PR6053.A73L68   1988
823'.914—dc19   88-15189
ISBN 0 14 01.0851 3

Printed in the United States of America by
R. R. Donnelley & Sons Company, Harrisonburg, Virginia
Set in Sabon

LOVE

One day, Annabel saw the sun and moon in the sky at the same time. The sight filled her with a terror which entirely consumed her and did not leave her until the night closed in catastrophe for she had no instinct for self-preservation if she was confronted by ambiguities.

It had happened as she walked home through the park. In the system of correspondences by which she interpreted the world around her, this park had a special significance and she walked along its overgrown paths with nervous pleasure, especially in certain yellow, tarnished lights of winter when the trees were bare and the sun, as it set, rimmed the branches with cold fire. An eighteenth-century landscape gardener planned the park to surround a mansion which had been pulled down long ago and now the once harmonious artificial wilderness, randomly dishevelled by time, spread its green tangles across the high shoulder of a hill only a stone's throw from a busy road that ran through the city dockland. All that remained of the former mansion were a few architectural accessories now the property of the city museum. There was a stable built on the lines of a miniature Parthenon, housing for Houyhnhnms rather than natural horses; the pillared portico, especially effective under the light of a full moon, never to be entered again by any horse, functioned only as a pure piece of design, a focal point in the green composition on the south side of the hill where Annabel rarely ventured for serenity bored her and the Mediterranean aspect of this part of the park held no excitements for her. She preferred the Gothic north, where an ivy-covered tower with leaded ogive windows skulked among the trees. Both these pretty whimsies were kept securely locked for fear of the despoliation of vandals but their presence still performed its original role, transforming the park into a premeditated theatre where the romantic imagination could act out any performance it chose amongst settings of classic harmony or crabbed quaintness. And the magic strangeness of the park was enhanced by its curious silence. Footfalls fell softly on the long grass and few birds sang there, but the presence all around of the sprawling, turbulent city, however muffled its noises, lent such haunted, breathless quiet an unnatural quality.

The park maintained only a single, still impressive entrance, a massive pair of wrought-iron gates decorated with cherubs, masks of beasts, stylized reptiles and spearheads from which the gilding flaked, but these gates were never either open or closed. They hung always a little ajar and drooped from their hinges with age; they served a function no longer for all the railings round the park were gone long ago and access everywhere was free and easy. The park was on such high ground it seemed to hang in the air above a vast, misty model of a city and those who walked through it always felt excessively exposed to the weather. At times, all seemed nothing but a playground for the winds and, at others, an immense drain for all the rain the heavens could pour forth.

Annabel went through the park in a season of high winds and lurid weather, early one winter's evening, and happened to look up at the sky.

On her right, she saw the sun shining down on the district of terraces and crescents where she lived while, on her left, above the spires and skyscrapers of the city itself, the rising moon hung motionless in a rift of absolute night. Though one was setting while the other rose, both sun and moon gave forth an equal brilliance so the heavens contained two contrary states at once.

Annabel gazed upwards, appalled to see such a dreadful rebellion of the familiar. There was nothing in her mythology to help her resolve this conflict and, all at once, she felt herself the helpless pivot of the entire universe as if sun, moon, stars and all the hosts of the sky span round upon herself, their volitionless axle.

At that, she bolted from the path through the long grass, seeking cover from the sky. Wholly at the mercy of the elements, she lurched and zig-zagged and her movements were so erratic, apparently at the whim of the roaring winds, and her colours so ill-defined, blurred by the approaching dusk, that she might herself have been no more than an emanation of the place or time of year.

At the crest of the hill, she flung up her hands in a furious gesture of surrender and pitched herself sideways off the path, concealing herself behind a clump of gorse where she lay moaning and breathless for a few moments. The wind tied strands of her hair to spikes of gorse and thus confirmed her intuition that she should not budge one inch until the dreadful, ambiguous hour resolved itself entirely to night. So there she stayed, a mad girl plastered in fear and trembling against a thorn bush suffering an anguish which also visited her when pressed just as close to the blond flesh of the young husband who slept beside her and did not know her dreams, although he was a beautiful boy whom anybody else would have thought well worth the effort of loving.

She suffered from nightmares too terrible to reveal to him, especially since he himself was often the principal actor in them and appeared in many hideous dream disguises. Sometimes, during the day, she stopped, startled, before some familiar object because it seemed to have just changed its form back to the one she remembered after a brief, private period impersonating something quite strange, for she had the capacity for changing the appearance of the real world which is the price paid by those who take too subjective a view of it. All she apprehended through her senses she took only as objects for interpretation in the expressionist style and she saw, in everyday things, a world of mythic, fearful shapes of whose existence she was convinced although she never spoke of it to anyone; nor had she ever suspected that everyday, sensuous human practice might shape the real world. When she did discover that such a thing was possible, it proved the beginning of the end for her for how could she possess any notion of the ordinary?

Her brother-in-law once gave her a set of pornographic photographs. She accepted the gift absently, without doing him the courtesy of investigating the complex motives behind it, and she examined the pictures one by one with a certain impersonal curiosity. A glum, painted young woman, the principal actress (torso and legs sheathed in black leather, sex exposed) eyed the camera indifferently as though it were no business of hers she was blocked at every orifice; she went about her obscene business with neither relish nor disgust, rather with the abstract precision of the geometrician so that these stark juxtapositions of genitalia, the antithesis of the erotic, were cold as Russia when nights are coldest there and possessed chiefly the power to affront. Annabel, comforted and reassured by these indifferent arrangements of bizarre intersecting lines, became convinced they told a true story. For herself, all she wanted in life was a bland, white, motionless face like that of the photographic whore so she could live a quiet life behind it, because she was so often terrified when the pictures around her began to move, as she thought, of their own accord and she could not control them.

So these photographs were cards in her private tarot pack and signified love.

As she waited for the sun to set, she had ample time to refresh and embellish her initial terror and was finally seized with the conviction that this night, of all nights, it would never disappear at all but lie stranded for ever above the horizon so she would have to stay nailed to the hillside. At these times, she thought of her husband as a place of safety although, when she was face to face with him, she could find no means of telling him her fears since his brother was her only intermediary between her private experience and the common one; and, this time, it was

4

he who rescued her so she learned to trust him a little more.

But when she first met the boy who became her brother-in-law, he frightened her more than anything had done until that date.

Before they were married, when she was living with Lee, who was then a student, Lee came home from a lecture one February afternoon to find his brother had returned from North Africa unannounced. The newcomer sat on the floor at right angles to the wall in the recesses of a black, hooded, Tunisian cloak which concealed every part of him but for long fingers which drummed restlessly against his knee. On the other side of the room, Annabel sat in a similar position, shielding her face with her hair. An air of mutual mistrust filled the room. Lee dropped a string bag containing groceries on the floor and went to feed the dying fire.

'Hi, Alyosha,' said Buzz.

Lee knelt beside him to hug and kiss him.

'I have a dose,' enunciated Buzz with precision.

'You want to eat?'

Buzz padded after Lee into the adjoining kitchen and, grasping him from behind, pressed his fingertips against the base of Lee's throat until Lee went limp.

'I don't like her,' said Buzz and released him.

When Lee could speak, he said: 'Try that unarmed combat stuff on me again and I'll smash you against the fucking wall.'

'Bad . . .' said Buzz effortfully . . . 'vibes . . .'

Lee shrugged and broke eggs into a pan of hot fat.

'But I don't like her!' wailed Buzz childishly. He wound the cloak round himself to hide. 'And you're knocking her off, aren't you; you're screwing her all night.'

Lee menaced him briefly with the breadknife and he fell back, whimpering, for knives, his favourite weapon, impressed him horribly when they were turned against him. He crouched on the floor like a dog to eat his food in the tent of the black cape and Annabel still sat where they had left her, in the dark.

'That's my brother,' said Lee pleasantly.

'What's wrong with him?'

'Gonorrhoea.'

'Pardon?'

'A venereal disease,' explained Lee.

'Apart from that.'

'He's a freak.'

She appeared to consider this gravely for a few minutes. Then she said: 'Come here.'

She embraced Lee with such unexpected passion he started to shiver, murmuring her name and running his hands over her body. As they toppled sideways to the floor, the lights in the room flashed on and Buzz's shadow fell over them like that of an avenging angel for he spread out his arms so the folds of the cloak made wings. He attacked them both impartially and, catching Lee unprepared, soon succeeded in subduing him; when he adopted the traditional pose of the victor, his knee in Lee's belly, he snarled:

'Don't ever let me catch you at it again!'

But time passed and Buzz and Annabel became, in a sense, accomplices and then they left Lee out of their plottings for he understood neither of them, although he loved them both.

Buzz never went out without a camera; that night of January, when he found her on the hill, he took several photographs of her without her knowledge as soon as he saw her angular, familiar body stretched out against the bush in the strange light. Then he knelt beside her without speaking till there was nothing but honest moonlight before he led her home to the flat in a Victorian square, where they all three lived together. She stood in the dark porch fumbling for her latch-key with chilly fingers stiff with fright which could not find their way about the satchel which also contained her sketchbooks and a few things, a model soldier, three tubes of white gouache and a bar of chocolate, which she had stolen that day at lunchtime. Buzz dug into the bag and found her key, took the chocolate bar, kissed her cheek and ran off for he had arranged a party in the flat that night and had some preparatory business to do. He liked organizing parties for he always hoped something terrible would happen when so many people intersected upon one another. He was, as usual, in a state of suppressed nervous excitement.

In their room, Lee lay face down on the carpet in front of the fire, perhaps asleep. The walls round him were painted a very dark green and from this background emerged all the dreary paraphernalia of romanticism, landscapes of forests, jungles and ruins inhabited by gorillas, trees with breasts, winged men with pig faces and women whose heads were skulls. An enormous bedstead of dull since rarely polished brass, spread with figured Indian cotton, occupied the centre of the room which was large and high but so full of bulky furniture in dark woods (chairs, sofas, bookcases, sideboards, a round mahogany table covered with a fringed, red plush cloth, a screen covered with time-browned scraps) that one had to move around the room very carefully for fear of tripping over things. Heavy velvet curtains hung at the windows and puffed blue dust at a touch; a light powder of dust covered everything. On the mantelpiece stood the skull of a horse amongst a clutter of small objects such as clockwork toys, stones of many shapes and various bottles and jars.

All this heterogeneous collection seemed to throb with a mute, inscrutable, symbolic life; everything Annabel gathered around her evoked correspondences in her mind so all these were the palpable evidence of her own secrets and the room expressed a hermetic spiritual avarice. In her way, she was a miser. In this oppressive room, Lee was as out of place as a goatherd's son trapped in a witch's house for he always took about with him a peasant or rustic breath of open air. He lay on the carpet and traced the threadbare warp with his finger. She moved almost silently but he heard her come in and raised his head. His eyes were of the clearest, most beautiful, most intense blue though always rimmed with reddish inflammation. He put out his hand and caught hold of one of her naked feet, which were both caked with damp earth from the hillside.

'Trampling in graves again,' he said for he took her other-worldliness lightly. 'Oh, my duck, you'll catch your death.'

The local evening newspaper drifted apart leaf from leaf in the draught caused by Annabel's entrance. Lee trapped the paper and pointed out a blurred photograph.

'Joanne. Joanne Davis. She's in my form at school. I teach her. Sweet Jesus, can you credit it?'

He was a schoolteacher for a living and worked in a comprehensive school. His pupil was a buxom blonde who wore a bikini with a sash over her bosom identifying her as the winner of a minor beauty contest. She revealed her teeth in a smile as brilliantly artificial as those of acrobats.

'She has no academic bent,' said Lee. 'Sixteen, she is. I'm an old man to her. I'm Mr Collins and sometimes even "sir".'

He was twenty-four, old enough for this to sadden him, but Annabel indifferently stirred the paper with her toes. She was so full of the terror of the park she could barely think of anything else and she rehearsed the simple sentence carefully before she asked him if supper was ready so that no tremor in her voice should betray her agitation. He nodded and abandoned the attempt to chat with her; they did not speak to one another, much. She evaded his hands and padded out into the kitchen to inspect the food he had prepared in case it contained snakes and spiders while Lee rose and found her antique lace tablecloth in the drawer of an enormous sideboard which was decorated with small, carved lions' heads with brass rings in their noses. He did not hear her return but saw her suddenly materialize in the dusty surface of the sideboard mirror, which was subtly warped, so her face looked as if it were reflected in water. All was as it should be in the kitchen and she gave him a smile of such unexpected sweetness that he turned, put his arms around her and hid his face in her hair, for he was having an affair with another woman, as was only to be expected.

'What did you do today, love?'

'I drew the model,' she said indifferently.

Her apparent indifference to the world outside her own immediate perceptions had ceased to hurt Lee but never failed to bewilder him for he always tried to be as happy as he could, himself. They had lived together for three years but still, when he was with Annabel, Lee was like a lone explorer in an unknown country without a map to guide him. Genuine explorers rarely smile for what they have undergone wipes the smiles from their faces for good; Lee was not yet quite ready to join that select and aristocratic company but he was already very much changed from what he had been and his marvellous smile was a far less frequent event than in the days before he met her, for until then he had been perfectly free.

This freedom had been the result of an unusual combination of circumstances. Neither he nor his brother carried through life the name he had been born with. Lee had undergone three changes of forename, from Michael to Leon to his own choice of diminutive borrowed from some now forgotten Saturday-morning cinema Western, Lee, and he arrogantly retained the last name into adult life for he was not ashamed of his romanticism. The aunt who cared for both of the boys changed his name to Leon, for Trotsky. She was a remarkable woman, a canteen cook and shop steward who worked her fingers to the bone to support the two boys and inculcated in them a sense of pride and a certain critical severity which, in adulthood, they both expressed sufficiently in their separate ways, though neither in a way of which their aunt would have approved.

Buzz, however, had renamed himself. At four years old, he selected this mysterious monosyllable from the credits of a television cartoon film and after that he insisted it was his own name and his only name; he refused to answer to any other and so he soon acquired it permanently. He said he liked the word because it hung in the air for a long time after him but Lee guessed he liked the persistent irritation of the sound. Their aunt changed their original surname to her own by deed poll after their mother, her sister, forfeited her social personality in such a spectacular manner that she became a legend in the neighbourhood where they lived.

On Empire Day at the primary school which Lee attended when he was a small child, there was an annual festival with a display of flags, patriotic tableaux and country dancing. This celebration reached its climax when a selection of infants filed on to the playground in their best clothes with, attached by string, a card bearing a single letter around each neck so that, assembled in a line, they spelled out in total the motto of the school, a Kantian imperative: DO RIGHT BECAUSE IT IS RIGHT. Upon a blowing day in June, in his sixth year, Lee carried the letter S when his mother, naked and painted all over with cabbalistic signs, burst into the crowded playground and fell writhing and weeping on the asphalt before him.

When Lee attained the age of reason and acquired his aunt's pride, he was glad his mother had gone mad in style. There could be no mistaking her intention nor could her behaviour be explained in any other terms than the onset of a spectacular psychosis in the grand, traditional style of the old-fashioned Bedlamite. She progressed to unreason via no neurotic back alleyway nor let any slow night of silence and darkness descend upon her; she chose the high road, operatically stripping off her clothes and screaming to the morning: 'I am the whore of Babylon.' His aunt took him to visit her in hospital from time to time but she was beyond recall and failed to recognize them as if they had been, at the best of times, chance and unmemorable acquaintances. So, soon after they went to live with their aunt, she saw the logic of the child when the younger brother insisted on changing his name. She changed Michael's for him as well and blotted out the family name with her own.

In the street where the brothers lived with their aunt during their childhood, it always seemed to be Sunday afternoon. It is becoming increasingly difficult to find such streets, though they used to exist in large numbers in all our great cities – those quiet terraces of artisans' dwellings where the sunlight falls on cracked paving stones and smoky brick with a peculiar sweetness and the winds seem never chill nor boisterous. In summer, they hang protectors of faded canvas over the front doors to prevent the sun from peeling off still more of paint blistered already by suns of many summers and old men sit outside in shirtsleeves on kitchen chairs, as if put out to air upon the pavement. On the low window ledges, one might find, here, a pie set out to cool or a jelly to set, there, a dreaming cat; the windows themselves are hung with half-curtains of coarse lace or display dusty, unlifelike plants in green glazed pots and plaster Alsatian dogs, though now and then one catches glimpses of those tiny, brown front rooms flickering in the light of coal fires – rooms which, in winter, seem to promise all the warmth in the world. A gentle, respectable serenity pervades these scenes of urban pastorale. In such a street, behind scalloped lace, their aunt ferociously refused to submit to cancer in the style of a revolutionary, in a room full of yellowing pamphlets. It took her a whole, stifling, oppressive summer to die but all the time she died magnificently. That autumn, Lee went away to university and Buzz left London with him. The following year, the GLC pulled their old street down so all they had left was a few memories.

The brothers lived together in the university town. Lee was like a ploughboy and Buzz like a nightbird; Lee was sentimental while Buzz was malign; Lee's sensuality was equalled only by Buzz's perversity but they stayed together because they were alone in a world with which both felt themselves subtly at variance. Both walked warily, with the marvellous, collected walk of gunfighters of the Old West, and they were quick to take offence. They had the air of visitors who do not intend to stay long. Their mother's madness, their orphaned state, their aunt's politics and their arbitrary identity formed in both a savage detachment for they found such detachment necessary to maintain their precarious autonomy. From earliest childhood, they were accustomed to fighting, though Lee was better at it.

Lee was an honest orphan; his father had been a railwayman killed in the course of duty but after her husband's death, the wife had gone on the game and Buzz was fathered by an American serviceman who left behind him nothing but a crude, silver, finger-ring decorated with a skull and crossbones. Buzz created an authentic savage from this shadow. He became convinced the man had been an American Indian and claimed as proof his own straight, coarse, sooty hair, high cheekbones and sallow complexion. Sometimes the tribe he favoured most were the Apaches but, in less aggressive moods, he thought he might be a Mohawk since he had no fear at all of heights and often walked on roofs. Lee went to a grammar school but Buzz went to a secondary modern school. There, with a passionate stubbornness that earned his brother's unwilling respect, he steadfastly refused to learn anything useful.

He worked sporadically in factories, down at the docks or else serving or washing up in cafés. At the times he was not working, he lived off his brother and sometimes stole. He was taller than Lee and dressed himself in rags. He had neither talents nor aptitudes, only a disconcertingly sharp intelligence and a merciless self-absorption. He had long, thin hands as if expressly formed for picking and stealing and he bit his nails down to the half-moon. He lived at a conscious pitch of melodrama; once, filling out a form for some job or other he never achieved, he wrote down against the space marked: INTERESTS, the two words, sex and death.

'Don't let's exaggerate,' said Lee gently.

Lee looked like Billy Budd, or a worker hero of the Soviets, or a boy in a book by Jack London. He was of medium height and sturdy build; his eyes were blue and looked like the eyes of a seafarer partly because of the persistent slight reddening of the rims due to a chronic slum-child infection he did not shake off as he grew up. His hair was the colour of hay, his complexion fresh and only the lack of a front tooth took away the suspicion he might be simple-minded for it gave his gapped but dazzling smile a certain ambiguity. Like most people who happen to be born with a degree of physical beauty, he had become self-conscious very young in life and so profoundly aware of the effect of his remarkable appearance on other people that, by the age of twenty, he gave the impression of perfect naturalness, utter spontaneity and entire warmth of heart. 'Alyosha,' said Buzz with contemptuous admiration. 'Bloody Alyosha.'

Buzz's conversation was composed of unnerving silences interspersed with rare outbursts of intense but often disconnected speech. His huge, heavily lidded eyes (the irises large and dark, the pupils white and gleaming) were as disconcerting in his immobile face as if real eyes had moved within those faces the ancient Egyptians painted on their coffin lids. He had been grievously exposed to his mother's madness; her persistent delusion that her sallow, dark baby, child of a dark stranger, was touched with the diabolic, had warped his development to a certain extent and, besides, blighted him with a sense he might be cut out for some extraordinary fate though he had no idea what such a fate might be. But Lee bubbled with frank, engaging good humour though an air of alienation surrounded them; both appreciated they were exotics. They got on well together and it never occurred to either they might live apart.

They moved disinterestedly in the floating world centred loosely upon the art school, the university and the second-hand trade and made their impermanent homes in the sloping, terraced hillside where the Irish, the West Indians and the more adventurous of the students lived in old, decaying houses where rents were low. They were curiously self-contained so that people rarely mentioned them separately but always as the Collins brothers, like bandits. They knew of, and encouraged, this practice. But, the winter he was eighteen, Buzz disappeared precipitously to North Africa with a group of acquaintances leaving Lee to continue his studies alone in the flat they occupied at that time. They thought of this flat as another temporary place to stay awhile; in fact, they would find themselves living there for some years. It was to become their home.

This flat comprised two rooms separated by flimsy double doors and a kitchen, partitioned off by hardboard from the room at the front of the house. This front room, Lee's room, had long windows opening on to a balcony and, at that time, it was quite bare but for an alarm clock on the mantelpiece and a number of books cleverly stacked one on top of the other. He stored a mattress in a built-in cupboard, together with his clothes, and took it out at night to sleep on. It was a large room;

the walls and also the floorboards were painted white. The room echoed at the slightest sound or movement and Lee took off his shoes in the house, in the Japanese manner. Besides, he walked very quietly.

At that time, his room was always extraordinarily tidy, white as a tent and just as easy to dismantle but this was not ascetic barrenness. Because of its whiteness and uninterrupted space, the room was peculiarly sensitive to the time of day, to changes in the weather and to the seasons of the year. It changed continually and without any volition on Lee's part at all. There was nothing inside it to cast shadows but the movements of Lee himself and his brother, though the branches of the trees in the square outside shivered across this radiant interior in a variety of shadow shapes and, at night, the lights of the city played mysteriously across the endless walls. When he opened the window the winds rushed through.

Furnished entirely by light and shade, the characteristics of the room were anonymity and impermanence. There were no curtains at the windows for the room was so indestructibly private there was no need to hide anything, so little did it reveal. In this way, Lee expressed a desire for freedom; in the last years of his adolescence, freedom was his grand passion and a principal condition of freedom, it seemed to him, was lack of possessions. He also remained cool and detached in his dealings with women for freedom from responsibilities was another prerequisite of this state. So his sentimentality found expression in the pursuit of a metaphysical concept of liberty. When he was thirteen and Buzz eleven, he persuaded his brother to run away with him to Cuba to fight for Castro. Buzz stole a Spanish phrase-book from W. H. Smith's and they got as far as Southampton before the police found them. Their aunt was furious but gratified. The act was principally the expression of a sentimentality so pure it became his greatest virtue, in one sense, since his sentimentality often, when he grew up, made him act against his desires.

Buzz sent Lee some hash wrapped up in a djellabah from Marrakesh, for a Christmas present, and the brothers did not see one another for six months. During this time, Lee met the woman who later became his wife; on New Year's morning, he woke up on a strange floor to find an unknown young girl in his arms. She opened her eyes and some kind of hunger, some kind of despair in her narrow face caught at Lee's very tender heart. The room was full of darkness, silence and stale air. On a sofa, a young man and a girl twined together under a Paisley shawl; he murmured in his sleep and then a mouse rattled across the floor. Lee's unexpected visitor turned her head sharply at the noise, shivered and wept. He took her home with him and gave her some breakfast. When she told him her name was Annabel he knew at once she was middle-class and, by her nervous manner, he guessed she was a virgin.

Annabel ate a little, drank her tea and covered her face with her hands so he could not watch her any more. Her movements were spiky, angular and graceful; how was he to know, since he was so young, that he would become a Spartan boy and she the fox under his jacket, eating his heart out. The Japanese peasantry had an awed respect for foxes, who, they believed, could enter a person's body either through the breast or else the space between the flesh of a finger and any one fingernail. When the fox was inside, it would harangue its host until he lost his reason but Lee felt no need to beware of her. He smiled at her, leaned across the table and drew her hands away from her face, a pale face, mostly eyes. When he found out how friendless she was, he took her to live with him.

She sat in his white, empty room all day gazing at the wall. At intervals, he fed her and caressed her. Then, one morning while he was at a lecture, she took her pastel crayons and drew a tree on the section of the wall at which she habitually stared. She drew with such conviction she must have been sketching the tree in her mind for a long time for it was a flourishing and complicated tree covered with flowers and many coloured birds. At that, Lee judged the time had come. As he guessed, she was a virgin. He fetched a towel to wipe away the blood. She asked, would it be any better when she was used to it? He replied, 'Yes, love, of course, love,' though the sight of her curiously pointed teeth disturbed him and when she asked in a voice of pure curiosity: 'Why should you want to do this to me?' he was bereft of an answer. All at once his strong and graceful young body seemed to him a fragile and unnecessary appurtenance; her eyes reflected him in strange contours and he could not tell whether she saw him as he thought he was or not or what it was she saw in him, with her huge eyes which too much weeping seemed to have given the shape of tears laid on their sides. He realized he could supply her only with a physiological answer while she would never be satisfied with less than an existential one and he became melancholy but she was full of questions and soon drew his hand to the region of her fresh wound although it was not passion which moved her but, perhaps, curiosity. This happened on a very cold day towards the end of January, when snow was falling outside.

Two months before he met her, she tried to commit suicide by taking an overdose of sleeping tablets but the warden of the hostel where she lived found her in time. At the hospital where she was taken, she exhibited such marked stress symptoms at the suggestion she leave the art school where she was a student and return to her parents that they judged it best to leave her exclusively under the warden's kindly eye. The warden was a liberal woman in her forties who hoped nothing better for Annabel than that at last she might find someone to love her. Her room-mate at the hostel took her to a party on New Year's Eve. Annabel sat by herself in a corner and looked, first at some old magazines she found on the floor and, next, at the figures before her in the candlelight. She saw a series of interesting conjunctions of shapes and one or two disturbing faces and then she went to sleep. She woke up again because she was cold.

It was so late that all the lights were out and the candles burned down to stubs. Most of the guests had gone though a couple were making love on a sofa and several others were sleeping on the floor. Annabel was so cold she arbitrarily selected one boy and went to lie down beside him to keep herself from freezing. 'Whom have we here?' he said in the morning. Later, the warden visited him and was, of course, charmed; she thought he was sweet-tempered and stable and happily confided Annabel to his care.

He did not expect her to stay with him but she did so. Soon she brought in a record player from her old room. As he had suspected, she liked baroque harpsichord music best of all. He called upon reserves of tact, gentleness and sensitivity formed during his aunt's last illness to cope with her vagarious moods; she was capable of every shade of melancholy from a sweet sadness to the bleakest despair. He was used to having somebody to care for and, because his brother was away, he cared for her. She slept beside him and occasionally, out of pure curiosity, embraced him. Sometimes he succeeded in eliciting a small, tremulous response from her but, more often, not, though he often woke in the mornings to find her, awake already, staring at him fixedly with her peculiarly luminous eyes as if blasting him with Platonic intimations he did not understand. Then his initial disquiet would briefly revisit him and he suspected that her visionary eyes pierced his disarming crust of charm to find beneath it some other person who was, perhaps, himself.

He was attracted to her because he was unsure of his effect upon her and became increasingly attached to her because of her strangeness which seemed to him qualitatively different but quantitively akin to the strangeness he himself felt, as though both could say of the world: 'We are strangers here.' Fish in the deep sea are luminous so that they can recognize one another; might not men and women also exude some kind of speechless luminescence to those akin to them? He felt a sense of unspoken contact with her, like that of two people from different countries who do not speak one another's language thrust together in a third whose language neither understands. Besides, for the first month they lived together, he was sleeping with the wife of his philosophy tutor, although it took him several years to realize that a logical remedy for some of his and Annabel's discontents might be the presence of a complacent third, and a disaster to understand, still later, that it was not an entirely satisfactory solution.

This woman was perhaps five years older than Lee and he felt a certain derisive affection for her, though he continued with the affair because he was sure he was irrelevant to her and their experience appeared to cross over one another's in a perfectly abstract manner with no recognition of each other's individual natures. She was a tiny, sullen brunette, the mother of three small children. She had the gritty texture of the chronically unhappy and treated the young lover she had acquired out of spite and boredom with savage contempt, except for certain glimpses of her all-consuming discontent as she clung to him in the aftermath. 'It is like screwing the woman's page of the *Guardian*,' he told Buzz but he never mentioned her to anyone else out of indifference rather than discretion.

She made cool and practical arrangements. He went to see her twice a week, in the afternoons, when her children were at their play group and also on Thursday evenings, when they were in bed and her husband took an evening class on the concept of mind. They always made love in the spare room on a sheetless bed under a framed reproduction of a Picasso blue-period harlequin with a bloom of dust on the glass. During the entire course of the affair, she never solicited so much as a single piece of information from Lee concerning his family, his environment or his ambitions; she showed no curiosity of any kind about him at all. He thought this was very interesting.

Anyway, she was a great convenience for him; he took a certain pleasure in coupling with the wife of a man who taught him ethics; she left most of his evenings free; and he felt, with a puritanical sense of satisfaction inherited from his aunt, that he was learning something important about the middle class. But when he arrived one Thursday evening in early February, he found her in a filthy mood and followed her, with a more than usually wary tread, into the terra incognita of the living room.

Unknown but by no means unpredictable. On a guard before

the fire, small garments steamed. He saw she had been reading *The Second Sex*, which lay face down on the floor. The walls were beige, a cerebral Modrian print hung over the home-made hi-fi and bits of plastic toy scattered the rush matting. Lee gave himself his private grin of wry pleasure, a facial expression he preferred to conceal from the world most of the time in case it gave too much away.

The weather remained cold; he squatted down on the matting and warmed his hands at the fire. He wondered if he should buy some rush matting for Annabel lay full length on the cold, hard boards for hours on end and he often thought she looked as if she were on a slab in a morgue. He did not like to be a prey to such melodramatic imagery. His other love – that is if Annabel were to be defined as his lover – anyway the other woman – and was she the Other Woman or simply another woman? – anyway, this particular woman seated herself in an armchair and drew her legs up defensively beneath her, thus making herself impregnable. She wore jeans, a checkered shirt, her feet were bare and her long, dark hair was caught at the nape by a rubber band. She twirled her wedding ring around her finger, a sure sign of repressed annoyance, and she was mute.

Lee rocked back and forth on his heels, holding out his hands to the electric bars. Tonight, he looked like Barnaby Rudge. Mentally he wandered through his wardrobe of smiles, wondering which one to wear to suit this ambiguous occasion. At a very early age, Lee discovered the manipulative power of his various smiles and soon learned to utilize them in order to smooth his passage through life for he liked to have an easy time of it; that was what he called being happy. He selected a tentative and encouraging smile; it clicked into position so smoothly you would have sworn he wore his heart upon his face. As soon as the smile materialized, she burst into speech.

'You have shacked up with some bird, I hear,' she said.

'Yeah,' said Lee slowly, scenting trouble. 'So what?'

She made a dismissive gesture with her hands, got up and started to prowl around the room.

'Of course, I can hardly expect you to be faithful to me.'

'So that's it!' thought Lee and knew the affair was at an end. He chose his words carefully.

'I dunno. You've got every right to *expect* me to be faithful to you but whether I am or not, that's a different kettle of fish, isn't it?'

She continued to stalk around the room so stormily he became embarrassed for her as her behaviour seemed far in emotional excess of the circumstances.

'Why didn't you tell me yourself?'

'No business of yours.'

'Thank you,' she said ironically.

'Look,' said Lee. 'Something's biting you over and above me pulling a piece of stray.'

'To hear you talk, who would ever believe you were an undergraduate?'

At that, Lee decided to hurt her feelings.

'Here, are you scared I'll give you crabs or something, or some vile disease?'

When she kicked him with her naked foot, he realized this analysis was correct and, as he went sprawling, he began to laugh. This made her angrier than ever.

'Couldn't you have told me about this girl yourself?'

'I haven't got a talking mouth,' said Lee. He returned again to his oriental squat and turned upon her vengefully the full, disconcerting force of his dazzling smile for it had never occurred to him to tell her about Annabel since this other woman was so unimportant to him. Not that Annabel was, as yet, important to him. She lit a cigarette curtly, averting her head so as to regain her composure. It was a pleasant room, full of books and newspapers. Lee read a spine or two.

'You are quite irrelevant to me, a thing. An object. The first time I slept with you, it was an *acte gratuit*. An *acte gratuit*,' she repeated with some irritation for he did not seem to understand her. 'Do you know what I mean?'

Lee said nothing, out of spite.

'It was meaningless and absurd. It was a contentless act but, then, everything was contentless as if nothing cast any shadow, except my children and I couldn't communicate with them.'

She fell silent. Lee glanced at her from under his lashes, half sorry for her, half extremely irritated. The silence lengthened. At last he stood up.

'Well, I'd better be getting along,' he said.

'You're a rat,' she said. 'You rat.'

Lee wanted nothing except to get out of the house as quickly as he could and would have agreed to anything she said. He nodded briskly.

'Yeah, I'm a rat,' he said. 'A rat of working-class origins,' he amplified.

At that, she jumped up and pummelled him with her fists. He caught hold of her wrists and hit her once. She subsided immediately and touched her cheek wonderingly with her finger-tips.

'She's got funny eyes,' said Lee. 'I quite like her, if you want to know. She doesn't say much. And she'll probably have to go when my brother comes home, anyway.'

In moments of stress, his grammar-school accent collapsed completely. He was surprised to appreciate the extent of his agitation and also to hear his own words; since he never spoke anything but the truth, he must have become attached to Annabel. He was bewildered and blinked a little. Due to his chronic eye infection, his eyes watered under bright lights, weariness or strain; the lights were low but his eyes began to water. She pulled away her hands for the touch of his skin had become unbearable to her and gazed at him with wonder as she recalled his past physical tenderness. She was full of unbelieving pain to realize at last such caresses had been quite involuntary and, in a sense, nothing to do with her, no kind of tribute.

'What the fuck do you want from me, anyway?' demanded Lee with some brutality. 'You want me to ask you to leave your husband and come and live with me?'

'I'd never do that,' she said immediately.

'Well, then,' said Lee and sighed. At this time, he did not appreciate shades of meaning. He thought a door must either be open or closed and that, in general, people meant what they said. Besides, he was poor and could not have afforded to support her and her children, even if he had wanted to. His eyes were watering so badly the dark young woman before him shimmered.

'I could make things very unpleasant for you at the university,' she said.

Now it was his turn to be shocked.

'So it's true what my aunt told me about the duplicity of the bourgeoisie?'

Then the baby wailed and its mother gave a small shriek and twitched a little. Lee was filled with angry sadness.

'Ah, come off it,' he said. 'You had what you wanted, didn't you?'

'You have a cold heart, I must say.'

'What?'

'You lay me and you don't give two straws –' Her hair was coming loose from its band and her face was flushed.

'What is it that's troubling you, honestly, I mean, troubling you so much?'

'Go away,' she said. 'I feel degraded.'

Lee was deeply offended and demanded, shocked: 'Here, how can you possibly find sex degrading?'

She stopped short, taken aback, shot him a puzzled look and then took a deep breath.

'I could have you thrown out of the university.'

'Yeah, well,' said Lee slowly for he was beginning to realize she was attracted to him because she thought he was a thug. 'Yeah, well; then I'd come and beat you up, wouldn't I? Me and my bruvver, we'd both come.'

She had seen his brother in the street.

'Dear God,' she said. 'I really think you would.'

She might have wished, all the time, that Lee would fall in love with her to lend the whole encounter a little more significance but if this was so he did not realize it. It seemed to him she had used him as a screen on which to project her own discontents, a fair exchange. He had a simple sense of justice.

'Go away, Leon Collins,' she said.

Lee realized she had learned his name by glancing through her husband's class list for nobody ever called him Leon, not even his teachers, face to face. But, then, he did not know her first name, either. Diminishing screams of the still-untended baby followed him down the stairs.

'Well,' thought Lee, 'you live and learn.'

But he was very bewildered and extremely ill at ease. His room reverberated with harpsichord arpeggios. Annabel had let the fire die down to a few red coals so all was a glowing darkness intermittently punctuated by headlights of passing cars which flickered through the uncurtained windows to play like the aurora borealis on the body of the girl on the white floor, which was the only object to disturb the emptiness of the room but for her record player. The music ended and the needle hiccupped over vacant grooves. Lee went to switch it off and she caught his arm.

'You smell of outdoors,' she said. 'But you've been with some woman.'

'Well, yes and no,' said Lee, who always spoke the truth. 'Does it hurt your feelings?'

He spoke very gently because her distress was so impassive. She shook her head wordlessly and the tears came pouring down without a sound.

'Then why are you crying?'

'I thought you wouldn't come back.'

'Oh,' said Lee, nonplussed. Her huge, grey eyes were fixed on his face; his own eyes began to scald again as if burned by her metaphysical fire. He thought she was making some monstrous demand on him but he could not interpret it and, trapped in this strange regard, he found he was trembling so much he had to put out his hand to support himself on the floor. He was astonished to discover he was so touched by this grief, perhaps

23

because it seemed evidence he was important to her in some mysterious way he could not fathom. The longer he stared into her eyes, the greater grew his confusion until, at last, with both relief and fear, he saw her newly magic outlines were those of a thing that needed to be loved. He thought: 'Oh, God, I should have recognized her sooner.' So his stoic sentimentality betrayed him. He kissed her hesitantly and though she did not open her mouth she placed her hands on his shoulders underneath his heavy jacket. He shrugged off his coat and spread it out to shield her from the hard floorboards. She lay back compliantly and did not take her gaze from him so he was still trembling from her scrutiny as he entered her.

But, even if they now acknowledged the state of love, their lovemaking was still permeated by unease for she understood the play of surfaces only superficially; she was like a blind man at a firework display who can only appreciate the fires in the air by interpreting their various degrees of magnificence through the relative enthusiasms of the noisy crowd. The nature of the dazzlement was dimly apprehended, not known.

On his return, Buzz seethed with jealous fury for a long time. In structure, the flat was an L-shaped ballroom divided by double doors which now served as a wall but this wall was very thin and Buzz, in his narrow cot, could hear each word and movement the lovers made. Every night he lay sweating at the unmistakable creakings and groans, writhing as he imagined their unimaginable privacy. He pressed his dark face into the pillow, cursed them bitterly and slowly became obsessed with the idea of stabbing them both as they slept together. He lovingly fingered his Moroccan knife and watched them during the day while, at night, he swore and masturbated. Lee was aware of the tensions ravaging his brother but was soon too much preoccupied with tensions of his own to pay them any attention for he could not ignore there was no magic implosion of the flesh in Annabel. He could evoke from her only those faint sighs and shudders the sensitive and perverse membrane of his brother's ear transformed to shrieks and cries. She seemed to

24

grow more and more fascinated by the appearance of his face and body but she had no memory of skin to compare the feel of his skin with and seemed to like, best of all, the sensation of intimacy she experienced in bed with him; she had often read about such intimacy. She began a series of pictures of him. She drew her first picture the morning after their first authentic night, when certain implicit avowals had been made; in this picture, he looked like a golden lion too gentle to ever eat meat. Over the years, she drew and painted him again and again in so many different disguises that at last he had to go to another woman to find out the true likeness of his face.

When Buzz stole his first camera, the flat was given over entirely to the cult of appearances. Buzz used the camera as if to see with, as if he could not trust his own eyes and had to check his vision by means of a third lens all the time so in the end he saw everything at second hand, without depths. He developed and printed the pictures in his back room and pinned them on the walls until he was surrounded by frozen memories of the moment of sight; to have them in a condition where he could hold them in his hand gave him a sense of security. He took innumerable photographs of Lee and Annabel and obtained some relief by means of this kind of voyeurism so the atmosphere in their home grew less strained, though they often woke up in the morning to find him perched on the end of the bed, clicking away. And he padded round after them, continually catching them unawares, so they were caught in all manner of situations and often wore expressions of startled irritation in the completed photographs. Cardboard crates of prints and negatives slowly accumulated in Buzz's room.

Lee had two old photographs which were precious to him. Neither brother had anything left from their childhood besides these photographs. One showed a line of clean children carrying letters which together formed the exhortation: DO RIGHT BECAUSE IT IS RIGHT; the other was of a large, stern, middle-aged woman outstaring the camera with a brother on either side of her. She was their aunt. The brothers looked themselves already, though one was eleven and the other nine, and leaned back on their heels in characteristic, defensive/aggressive stance but the aunt stood straight enough to outface a battalion and shame them. Annabel looked at the photograph of the aunt and then at Lee. Putting her finger to his cheek, she removed a tear but he did not want her to think he was really crying.

'That's no authentic tear, love: my eyes, they water easily.'

In fact, this tear both was and was not authentic. His eye disease rendered his tears ambivalent. But, since he had the simple heart of one who boos the villain, when, as he often did, he found he was crying, he usually became sad. Whether his tears were the cause or the effect of a grief or if this grief, when it was experienced, would define itself to him as a reaction to some arbitrary stimulus such as the picture of the dead woman whom he had loved or as a reflection on common mortality – these were questions he had not yet chosen or chosen to need to ask himself. So he usually pretended he was not crying although he had the habit of crying easily.

These were his two iconic photographs, that of a child named Michael and that of a family group. Buzz gave him a picture of himself and Annabel in bed asleep and that made a third, an image of a lover. Lee and Annabel looked like Daphnis and Chloë or Paul and Virginia; Lee, tangled in her very long hair, lay in the crook of her naked shoulder for she was taller than he and they looked as beautiful and peaceful as if made in heaven for one another. Lee kept these photographs in an envelope with their three birth certificates and, later, his marriage certificate. But he could find no causal connection between his three photographed faces. The infant, the child and the adolescent or young man whose face was still so new, unused and incomplete seemed to represent three finite and disconnected states. Looking in the mirror, he saw the face of a stranger to any of them with features which had been filtered through his wife's eyes and subjected to so many modifications in the process that it was no longer his own. There seemed no connecting logic between the various states of his life, as if each had been attained, not by organic growth but by a kind of convulsive leap from condition to condition. He felt no nostalgia for the innocence he found upon his old, cast-off faces, only a fierce indignation he should ever have been innocent enough to surrender his freedom. For now his once desert room where he had lived as aridly alone as Crusoe on his island with only Buzz for a sullen, un-dutiful Friday – now this room was choked with things, painted out in thick, dark colours and filled with such a rich, sombre gloom one took a deep breath before stepping over the threshold, knowing one was about to plunge into another, heavier kind of air.

In this cavernous, mysterious room, he hugged her tightly for he knew that duplicity thrives on physical contact. Here, where she and her furniture were sunk together in the same dream, she had at least a shape and an outward form; she had the same status as a thing, as her sofa possessed, or her sideboard with the lions' heads. Here, she was an object composed of impervious surfaces. But when she walked beside him down the street in her randomly assembled clothes, she was quite wispy and tenu-ous, like a phantom rag-picker. She was tall and very thin. Her hands were long and the veins stuck out from them in thick bunches like the veins on the freckled hands of old women. Her feet, also, bulged with swollen and protuberant veins. Because of her meagre build, she seemed still taller than she was, a sparse, grotesquely elegant, attenuated girl with a narrow face and hair so straight it fell helplessly down around her as a mute tribute to gravity. She had prehensile toes that could pick up a pencil and sign her name. She stole.

Lee was horrified to find she stole. She stole food from supermarkets and books from bookshops; she stole paints, ink, brushes and small items of clothing. Her parents were wealthy and gave her a large allowance but still she stole and Lee had always regarded thievery as the legitimate province only of the poor. He thought it morally proper the poor should steal as much as they could but, since money was given one only in

27

order to buy things with and so keep the wheel of the economy in motion, then it was the duty of the rich (the hub of the wheel) to purchase as much as they were able. Nevertheless, she continued to steal in spite of his stern disapproval and this proclivity proved one of the many things she and her brother-in-law held in common.

They married when her parents found out she and Lee were living together. Lee had taken his final examinations, obtained a mediocre degree and registered with the university's department of education for a teacher training course. His brother greeted this action with snarling derision but Lee was forced to support his household, who were either unable or unwilling to support themselves. Annabel informed her parents of her change of address without giving them any further details and they assumed she shared a flat with another girl. She visited them occasionally and, towards the end of the summer, they happened to be passing through the city on the way to Cornwall and came ringing the door bell early one morning.

Buzz was awake and working in the dark room he had improvised from his own quarters. It was a warm day and he wore nothing but a pair of filthy white sailor trousers holed, here and there, with acid. His Apache or Mohawk hair hung past his shoulders and he reeked of incense and chemicals. He went to answer the door and found a man and a woman in casual, expensive clothes who smelled of soap and money, odours alien to him. Because of his perversity, he led them into Lee's room through his own, past walls papered with pictures of their only daughter frequently unclothed and often in the arms of a man but they managed to retain their equanimity although Buzz's room was packed full of his fetishes, which included knives, carcasses of engines salvaged from the scrapyard and all his tanks of chemicals. He had also boarded up the windows to keep the light out. If Lee's room was like a fresh sheet of paper, Buzz's was like a doodling pad but the many objects which filled it were so eclectic in nature and lay about so haphazardly where he had let them fall that it was just as difficult to gain any hints from it towards the nature of whoever lived there.

Though Lee's room was already less pristine than it had been. A forest of trees, flowers, birds and beasts had invaded the walls so Lee and Annabel lay together on the narrow mattress like lovers in a jungle. She had already bought a red plush sofa, a round table and a stuffed fox in a glass case so the general effect, since it was that of transition between one extreme state and its polar opposite, would have been peculiarly disturbing if Annabel's parents had not had eyes only for their daughter and the gardener's boy, the covers pushed off them for the heat, sleeping.

'Wake up,' said Buzz. 'It's her mum and dad.'

Annabel shivered but stayed fast asleep. Lee, however, prised open his seccotined eyes and gave his tribute of tears to the glorious morning. When he saw a man in a dark suit looking down at him, he thought the worst had happened and it was a plain-clothes man come to look for hash or appropriated property. He rolled over and extended his wrists.

'It's a fair cop,' he said.

Immediately they took Annabel away with them and the brothers sat brooding in a room which seemed so under-furnished without her they knew they both would not be at ease in it again until her return. They felt incomplete without her presence; without any conscious volition of her own, by a species of osmosis, perhaps, since she was so insubstantial, somehow she had entered the circle of their self-containment. When her parents discovered that Lee was a graduate, in spite of appearances, they decided he might be a rough diamond and became a little more conciliatory but they still refused to let him see her unless he married her which at last he agreed to do, out of pride. Her mother wanted a white wedding and a church.

'My aunt would turn in her grave,' said Lee.

It was finally arranged the wedding should take place in the registry office of the town in which the brothers lived. A date was fixed and a licence obtained. Annabel remained with her parents in the Home Counties for the interim period and the brothers stayed where they were. As soon as he became aware that he was about to do something irreversible, Lee began to drink heavily for he could not have gone through with the marriage unless he passed the time before it in a state of oblivion. Annabel was quite incomprehensible to him and he already knew she was unbalanced; yet his puritanism demanded he should be publicly responsible for her. He was overcome with conflicting apprehensions.

*

One January morning, Annabel woke up and found it had been snowing so there was no apparent difference between the world outside and the world inside. Snow lay thickly on top of the wrought-iron curlicues of the balcony and caked the bare branches of the trees in the square; yet still the grey sky was full of soft, whirling flakes and every sound was silenced as if the snow pressed fingers in the ears. The room was full of white light reflected from outside and the only difference was that here it was not snowing for everything was as white as the extreme, unimaginable North except for the red enamel alarm clock, which now rang. Lee, still asleep, flung out one arm to depress the button; she took a technical pleasure in observing the musculature of his shoulders and the play of snowlight on the golden down which covered them for he was of a furry texture. He was colourful to look at and also reminded her of Canova's nude, heroic statue of Napoleon in Wellington House. She was grateful for his warmth. She watched the daily struggle to open his eyes and then he smiled to recognize her, hugged her, kissed her cheek and rooted about on the white floor beside him for his discarded clothes. She was especially pleased when she caught a glimpse of his leonine left profile. She found him continuously interesting to look at but it hardly occurred to her the young man was more than a collection of coloured surfaces and she had never learned to think of herself as a living actor, anyway. She did not even think of herself as a body but more as a pair of disembodied eyes – when she thought about herself at all, that is. She was eighteen, secretive and withdrawn since childhood. Her favourite painter was Max Ernst. She did not read books. Lee got her breakfast and built up a roaring fire.

It was too snowy to think of going to the art school. She lay against his very white pillow and drank her tea peacefully. She had chosen an old white flannel shirt of his to wear in bed and he thought this wilful and perverse attire was a simple, sexual defence, for which he forgave her. It was unnecessary to have forgiven her for she did not know it defended her. Though she had shared a bed with him for three weeks, she never thought of it as a place for anything but sleeping in. Therefore she did not know she had anything to protect while Lee assumed all manner of virginal hedging on her part and, unconcerned, waited for her to make up her mind. He picked up his books, put on several layers of clothing and went out into the snow for he was a conscientious student. For a while she watched the flames in the grate. Then she crept from the bed and, like Bluebeard's wife, sneaked into the forbidden territory of Buzz's room, where the air struck damp and chill.

Even before it became officially a dark room, it was very dark for the window opened on to a blank wall and, since his avocation was trading, it was also cluttered up with many odd objects as well as his ongoing fetishes. Everything was cold, miserable and arbitrary, a rummage sale presided over by many pictures of Red Indians cut out of books.

'What is your brother like?'

'An Apache, sometimes.'

She wandered about picking things up and putting them down again. She examined Buzz's clothes which were kept spilling out of a tea chest, selected a ragged vest dyed purple and a pair of orange crushed-velvet trousers, took off Lee's shirt and donned these garments to find out what Buzz felt like or what it might feel like to be Buzz. But his old clothes felt like any other greasy and unwashed old clothes and she was disappointed. She already felt a vague interest in him, just as she felt more comfortable in his room than she did in Lee's, although she now returned to it for warmth. She opened his neat cupboard, took out the box of pastel crayons she kept on his shelf, knelt on the mattress and, out of boredom, began to draw the tree Lee so seriously misconstrued as, perhaps, a tree of life when it was more nearly related (for him, at least) to the Upas Tree of Java, the fabulous tree that casts a poisoned shade.

Lee came home at lunchtime, glowing with cold and his hair full of snow. Removing his shoes and socks in the kitchen, he padded silently into his room to find it strewed, still, with bedclothes and breakfast dishes and a figure, now on tiptoe, adding a gaudy parrot to the topmost branch of a colourful tree. Dark hair hung down the back of a familiar vest and for a moment he thought his brother was back unexpectedly but the draughtsmanship was infinitely superior to anything of which Buzz was capable and she turned to him, offering him an unemphatic smile.

'Well, well,' said Lee.

The crumbling pastels had showered the bed with polychromatic grit and Lee was annoyed to see such a mess, though pleased she had at last been sufficiently moved to do something, whatever it was. So he thought the time was right for, at the back of his mind, he had always intended to lay her some time or other. He knelt on the mattress beside her and put his arm around her waist. She took this for only another of the small caresses he often gave her. When he buried his face in the cool flesh of her belly, she pretended to herself she was preoccupied with the position of the parrot which, she judged, should have been, perhaps, an inch or two further to the left but this pretence could not protect her for long because he kissed her breasts and the red crayon dropped from her hand.

Seized with intimations of an invasion of privacy, she looked down at his rough blond head with bewilderment for the sensation of his touch had no effect on her. The castle of herself was clearly about to be invaded and, though the idea of it surprised her, the actual indifference of her response told her she would submit indifferently and she thought: 'Why not? Why not?'

She made no effort to undress herself, to see what he would do, so he took his brother's clothes off her; he had to raise her limp arms to draw off the vest and part her legs to remove the trousers. She watched him all the time without appreciating the extraordinarily erotic effect of her passivity, her silence and her enquiring eyes, comforted by memories of the nursery because he undressed her as if she were a little girl. Then he took off his own clothes. She was half perplexed and half amused at the sight of his erection but somehow affronted by his general air of insouciance for she knew this was supposed to be an event of some significance for her. He lay down beside her again and she examined his face for some indication of what he would do next. He seemed to expect some advance on her part so she tentatively put her arms around his neck, or perhaps she did this because she had read somewhere, in a magazine, perhaps, that this was what she was supposed to do. She would have liked some instructions on how to behave for it is a hard thing to make love when one has few, if any, ideas of common practice. He seemed to be experiencing some private kind of pleasure from these contacts of surface upon surface and the interaction of skin and she bemusedly resented his privacy since she felt privacy was her exclusive property and nobody else had much right to it. When he kissed her, she knew enough to open her lips and allow him to explore the interior of her mouth; at the soft pressure of his tongue on her own, she let out a muffled, involuntary moan which was, rather, a question although Lee paid it no heed and nudged open her legs with his knee. She made no movements either of complicity or denial and was surprised how mysterious his actions were when he put his hand between her legs.

Then, unexpectedly, they had a conversation. He asked when she would have her next period and she told him, in two or three days' time, and he said: that's perfectly splendid, ducks, and gave her an honest and unpremeditated smile. In the deep focus of the embrace, he was more interesting to look at than she would ever have imagined and this never previously encountered smile enchanted her so much she kissed him of her own accord. She felt rather than saw his pleasure when she did so and this bewildered her even more for she was accustomed only to seeing.

'Here,' he said, 'you won't get much out of it this time, probably, but I'll try not to hurt you. Anyway' (he added puritanically) 'you ought to have had it by your age; whatever do they teach you at them schools.' She felt it served him right when she saw he was nonplussed at so much blood.

Lee wondered if it were one of those cases, well-known in medical literature, where rupture of the hymen brought on a fatal haemorrhage? And still she could not understand the function of it, nor see how, with one thing and another, he began to be very much afraid though she soon saw she could hurt him as badly with her silences as he could ever afflict her by any other means. After the blood dried, she also learned that, if she concentrated very hard, the touch of his hand released infrequent but marvellous images inside her head. So she gazed at him with wonder, as if he might be magic, and he looked at her nervously, as if she might not be fully human.

They rolled all over the pastel crayons scattered on the sheets so her back was variegated with patches and blotches all the colours of the rainbow and Lee was also marked everywhere with brilliant dusts, both here and there also darkly spotted with blood, each a canvas involuntarily patterned by those workings of random chance so much prized by the surrealists.

She was fortunate in her first lover in so far as he was kind, gentle and experienced; she was unfortunate in that soon he began to love her and, after that, could not leave her alone. As for Annabel, she was like a child who reconstructs the world according to its whims and so she chose to populate her home with imaginary animals because she preferred them to the drab fauna of reality. She quickly interpreted him into her mythology but if, at first, he was a herbivorous lion, later he became a unicorn devouring raw meat and she never saw him the same

34

twice, nor did these pictures have any continuity except for the constant romanticism of the imagery. She had no control over them, once they existed. And, as she drew him, so she saw him; he existed for her only intermittently.

Waking in the middle of the night, she sometimes saw white birds, perhaps albatrosses, frozen in the middle of the ceiling; if she could not make out their outlines, precisely, that made them even more terrifying and there was no comfort to be got from the man sleeping beside her for he had undoubtedly become another, some other thing. She lay immobile under the covers listening to the menacing thunder of his breathing and did not dare stretch out her hand to touch him for fear of encountering the leathern surfaces of a dragon's wing. One night Lee woke in the grip of a dream and reached out for her while she was asleep. She screamed so loudly Buzz sprang awake and darted to defend her.

'I thought you were an incubus,' she said to Lee when the ensuing confusion had died down. Then they had to make tea and so on, in the false cheerfulness of five in the morning. Still, whatever he was, he grew necessary to her and she even played with the idea of bearing his children, though these children existed solely in the terms of her mythology, were purely symbolic and quite undemanding, related not to fantasies of motherhood but to certain explicit fantasies she had of totally engulfing him which she occasionally experienced with extraordinary intensity when he penetrated her, as if, drawing him through her hairy portals, he could be forever locked up inviolably inside her, reduced himself to the condition of an embryo and, by dissolving in his own sperm, become himself his own child. So, by impregnating her, he would cease to exist.

Because she gave Lee so large, if so ambiguous, a role in her mythology, she wished, gently, to reduce him to not-being.

She allowed her parents to take her away but she knew she would come back in the end. It was all the same to her whether she married Lee or not though he regarded it as a legal contract. Her parents bought her a white dress to be married in but she forgot to put it on that morning and dressed herself as usual in jeans and tee shirt, although her mother made her change her clothes and brushed out her hair for her. Annabel stood beside her parents in front of the registry office, kicking at the plaster in the wall with a bored air, wearing a thin, pretty dress of white silk she had not chosen for herself while she waited for things to continue as they had done before. It was a hot day in July and the courtyard was full of the suave perfume of lime trees. The mother wore a suit of coffee-coloured lace. Lee was twenty minutes late, blanched, shaking and still fairly drunk. The ragged brother sat cross-legged outside during the ceremony as immobile as a veritable Apache with his camera slung round his neck like a talisman.

'Oh, my darling,' said Annabel's mother. 'It's not what I would have wished for you.'

Lee wrote his name in the register.

'What an unusual name,' said the mother with a faint note of hope. 'Leon.'

Lee realized that if they were foreign, some of their eccentricities might be excused so he bared his teeth in a snarl and said: 'I was named for Trotsky, the architect of the Revolution.'

At that, he remembered his aunt and thought his heart might break as he stood in the cool, bright building for he had abandoned all the hopes with which his aunt had named him, if he had ever understood them at all. 'Betrayed to the bourgeoisie!' he thought and, once outside, lurched against the wall as if to face the firing squad. The brilliant morning shot him through the eyes with darts of glass and he was crushed by the conviction that he had done something irreparable. He saw the man and the woman grimacing at his brother and his new wife, their daughter, and all transmitted signs and messages not one of which any of the others could interpret. Words flew out of their mouths like birds, up and away, and all were behaving well, even Buzz, though he looked fresh from a visit to the tomb of Edgar Allan Poe for he had found a black suit somewhere.

No wonder the daughter saw only appearances. Despite the

eccentricity of his behaviour, the uncouthness of his accent and the length of his hair, the parents were so impressed at the sight of the camera they thought Buzz might be a respectable Bohemian and would, one day, grow rich for they had read how photographers were the new aristocracy. So the camera was sufficient justification for the boy's wild appearance and both cast strained glances at the drunk, sick and shattered bridegroom as if they thought their daughter had made the wrong choice, if she was going to marry into Bohemia anyway, that is, and since she was so good at art, they might as well resign themselves. After all, they had let her go to art school. But Lee looked like a seaman after a week's leave in a rough port and could be incorporated into no tender system of dreams or hopes. Annabel lifted up her hand which wore a wedding ring. The morning fell apart. Overcome with nausea, Lee ran inside the registry office. He found the lavatory and vomited for a long time.

When he crept back nervously into the sunshine, shielding his hurt eyes with his hand, he found his abrupt departure had broken the frail bond of the wedding group who now stood each one far apart from the others and looked abstractedly outwards in different directions. The white carnation in the father's buttonhole would have brought tears to Lee's eyes if his eyes had not been full of tears already.

'You're covered in white,' said Buzz. 'How bridal, how apt.'

'There was a window.'

'I suppose you tried to climb through it and run away, then.'

'You bet.'

Buzz laughed and brushed the whitewash off Lee's shoulder. Lee was white as the plasterwork and running with sweat but he said: 'Nothing personal, love,' to Annabel and she took hold of his clammy hand where her parents had insisted he, too, should wear a ring.

Soon the parents drifted wanly away and the Collinses, now legally augmented by their third, returned to their quarter, up the hill, past the university, attracting to them a procession of chance acquaintances on the way so the boisterous party which arrived at the house was more Réné Clair than Antonioni and Lee, who thought it was immoral to be unhappy, soon regained his good humour. But that night Buzz had a paranoid *crise* because he smoked too much and Lee fought with him for about an hour, to keep him still.

Annabel folded herself up in a corner in her wedding dress which was very grubby by now and covered her ears with her hands for Buzz was screaming dreadfully. The light was that of a church at Christmas for they had lit a great many candles and the flickering room smelled of melted wax. The people who came to celebrate the wedding drifted out into the night for most of them knew from experience to leave the brothers well alone when they were wrestling with demons and, at last, Lee got a handful of sleeping tablets down Buzz's throat, half led and half dragged him to the safety of his narrow cot and held him till he went to sleep.

Annabel, altogether too white and sinister in the soft light, was slowly blowing out the candles one by one. Because of the indifference natural to her, Lee thought she showed no interest in what had happened to Buzz though she might have been too frightened to want to speak of it. However, he was too embarrassed at so much hysteria to do anything but act as if nothing out of the ordinary had occurred. Besides, she would have to get used to that sort of thing, if she was to live with them for ever. They went to bed together and it was no better and no worse than any other time except that Lee found it more difficult than usual, for he remembered that a door can be only open or closed and he had made some formal promises, before witnesses, that he ought not to sleep with any other woman again until the end of his natural life which meant, perhaps, another forty years. Unless Annabel died. Barricaded behind her immobility, Annabel felt nothing but forgot the wedding ceremony almost immediately. Next morning, she started to paint the walls dark green.

*

In the rich, dark room his touch told her he could not deceive her but she said: 'If you deceive me, I'll die,' and he hugged her more closely, on the brink of treacherous tears, for she did not even suspect him after they had lived together for so long. She would as soon have thought that her coronation mugs, her Staffordshire pottery figure of Prince Albert and her brass bedstead itself be unfaithful to her or her own clothes commit adultery. He occupied the most important place among these possessions she had bought at auction sales or which Buzz obtained for her; they went to the city tip together, too, and raked through ashes for objects. And they went out stealing while Lee was at work, to come home with their arms full of things, many of them useless.

Lee deluded himself that, since he was not emotionally involved with the girl, Carolyn, he was not, significantly, unfaithful to his wife. In the period of introspection which followed the inevitable catastrophe, he had ample time to ironically applaud the extent of his self-deceit but now he had neither the time nor the inclination to do so nor any intimation a catastrophe might be near for he thought that he had finally established an equilibrium and now things could go on for ever.

'Sleeping with Annabel is like reading Samuel Beckett on an empty stomach,' he said to Carolyn as he walked her home through deserted streets in the small hours. Though he spoke primarily to clarify the situation to himself and so excuse it (for he felt some premonitions of guilt) it came through to her as a seduction speech; it interested her in him. When they reached her room, he blinked at the light and inspected her posters and paper flowers curiously. He had forgotten how far Annabel's gloomy interior deviated from a young girl's norm. Momentarily embarrassed, Carolyn halted with her fingers on the fastening of her fur jacket, for something in his manner suggested that though they had returned to her room with only one purpose, the act seemed too intimate to be performed by people so unfamiliar to one another.

'Do right because it is right,' thought Lee but the motto was no help at all since it only implied the question of the nature of the right.

She laughed out of embarrassment and enquiry; the space between them vanished immediately. Contentless sexuality is the most puritanical of all pleasures since it is pure experience devoid of any extrasensory meaning and Lee suddenly appreciated the iron will of the wife of his tutor in ethics, who had been strong enough to evade the perils of the aftermath in which confidences may be exchanged and information gathered. Carolyn told him how she was in love with someone who was in love with some other person and, in return, he felt bound to offer her a few behavioural snapshots of Annabel, such as Annabel drawing her deceitful tree that winter morning; Annabel flipping his penis between her fingers and asking, 'What is it for?' and Annabel being beaten. But he realized these were not so much pictures of actual events, even though they had all happened, but somehow the terms in which he was forced to describe them turned them into stills from expressionist films, stark, grotesque and unnatural. So he talked a little more, though, by trying to formulate and coherently relate the exact truth about certain aspects of their relationship, he inflated these details out of all proportion and, as soon as he showed her Annabel being beaten, he knew he had gone too far.

He and Annabel sometimes played chess for she liked to handle the pieces of a red and white Chinese ivory set that Buzz had somehow acquired for her; she would fall into a reverie, her eyes fixed vacantly on the board caressing the knight or castle in her hand while Lee gnawed his fingernails and waited for some startling, irrational move which would throw his mathematical attack into disarray.

'She plays chess from the passions and I play it from logic and she usually wins. Once, I took her queen and she hit me.'

Though, he recalled, not sufficiently brutally to require that he tie her wrists together with his belt, force her to kneel and beat her until she toppled over sideways. She raised a strangely joyous face to him; the pallor of her skin and the almost miraculous lustre of her eyes startled and even awed him. He was breathless with weeping, a despicable object.

'That will teach you to take my queen,' she said smugly. There were bruises on her shoulders and breast when she took off her sweater to go to bed. She stroked herself thoughtfully and suggested: 'I should like a ring with a moonstone in it.'

Her transparency astonished him but he was guilty enough to go and look for a moonstone ring the next day. But there were no moonstones to be bought in the city so he found her a print of Millais' 'Ophelia' in a second-hand shop because Annabel often wore the same expression and she seemed surprised and contented enough with that, though he suspected she bore him a concealed grudge.

'What was she doing?' asked Carolyn. 'Was she trying to humiliate you?'

'Maybe. It's a roundabout way of doing it, though.'

Already he felt remorse that he had told this story in such a way that he himself appeared in a good light, for so he betrayed Annabel when he did not know who she thought he was when he beat her. As he returned home, the street lights were winking out and the birds singing. He often went out without Annabel and came home late for his friends bored her but this time she woke up as he slid into the bed and said: 'I had a bad dream. It was morning and you weren't here and were never coming back.' He closed his eyes and pressed his face into the pillow but could not forbear to take hold of her terrible, hot, sticky hand for he knew he was her only friend although she did not like him much.

'Sometimes I surprise her in front of a mirror, practising smiling,' Lee told his new mistress and it was true, as far as it went, for he often found Annabel smiling to herself in the mirror and he could not think what else she might be doing if it was not practising how to smile.

'Oh, darling, she does sound a bitch,' said Carolyn with false lightness; she was not an imaginative girl.

His face went as blank as if all capacity for expression had dropped straight out of it and Carolyn learned, in that moment, that a woman in love can never afford to reveal what feelings she may have towards her lover's wife. This knowledge in itself would have been worth the emotional price of the whole experience to Carolyn but, by the end of the affair, she had acquired so much miserable information about men and women she almost decided to give up relationships for good for, if she fell in love with Lee to distract herself, the cure proved worse than the disease.

She was a student of English literature and knew both brothers by sight and by word of mouth; they had an attractive reputation of danger because Buzz was a petty criminal and all kinds of rumours went around about the three-cornered household. Carolyn saw the wife once or twice in the street and dismissed her from her mind for Carolyn was far prettier than Annabel, much more passionate and three times as comprehensible. She was not at all prepared for the overwhelming jealousy she began to feel for this shadowy figure. It was as if she found herself cast willy-nilly in the role of the Other Woman and now she had to learn the entire traditional script, no matter how crippling she found it to her self-esteem. So, much later the same evening that Annabel had been terrified by the sun and moon, Carolyn arrived at Lee's flat with some of her friends because Buzz was giving a party and Carolyn could use it as an excuse to infiltrate Lee's home.

Buzz stuck candles by their own grease on to every flat surface and Lee helped him, half in hopes the house would catch fire and burn down for Buzz had told him about the scene on the hill. He had tried to talk of it to Annabel, she could not or would not answer him and now he was in a mood of savage depression. Buzz, half naked, had covered himself in stripes of red and black greasepaint. He pushed Annabel's bed into a corner, cleared away enough of their common junk to make a dancing space and opened the double doors to create a single, large, L-shaped room. By the time Carolyn and her cover arrived, the party could be heard half a block away and the hosts were lost among the guests.

Annabel sat wrapped in a flowered silk shawl making right angles to the wall on her brass bed, still too frozen with fear to drink from the glass of red wine she held in her hand. When Lee felt her eyes upon him, he thought she was privately accusing him of hypocrisy and soon grew in the mood for violence. The brothers danced together, a put-on or come-on for which they were notorious, an exotic display. Loud music played. Carolyn detached herself from her group and edged down the room until she reached the long windows. She slipped the catch on one window and let in a breath of cold air which made the candle flames around her quiver and sent coruscating lights up and down the shining surface of her white satin dress. Lee saw her and was by now drunk enough to give her his most dazzling smile. Her principal distinguishing feature was an air of tranquil self-confidence and he thought it was both plausible and even inevitable she might light him out of Juliet's tomb into some kind of promised land.

Afterwards, the events of the night seemed, to all who participated in them, like disparate sets of images shuffled together anyhow. A draped form on a stretcher; candles blown out by a strong wind; a knife; an operating theatre; blood; and bandages. In time, the principal actors (the wife, the brothers, the mistress) assembled a coherent narrative from these images but each interpreted them differently and drew their own conclusions which were all quite dissimilar for each told himself the story as if he were the hero except for Lee who, by common choice, found himself the villain.

'You're crying,' said Carolyn, touched.

He did not bother to correct her. He stood by the window and looked out across the tops of the leafless trees to the few windows still left glowing in the houses on the other side of the square.

'We all stole a car, once. Well, it wasn't so much stealing, more like taking and driving away, they told me I was too timorous for authentic stealing. I opened the glove compartment and found a leaflet that promised you a thousand destinations. Think of that.'

Carolyn, mystified, could not see the point.

'What happened then?'

'We couldn't decide where to go,' said Lee and laughed.

Annabel glimpsed the nacreous shimmer of Carolyn's dress intermittently through the shoulders of the dancers. The music continued to play extremely loudly. Buzz, magnificently painted, sat briefly beside her.

'All right, are you?'

She nodded. They both watched Lee's leonine left profile bent over the head of the girl in white.

'She's done up like a bride,' said Annabel softly, so that nobody could hear her.

'Sure you're all right?' demanded Buzz, quivering in the expectation of disaster.

'Give me your ring.'

He slipped his father's silver ring on to her thin forefinger, the only one it would fit, and she allowed him a ghostly smile.

'Now I'm invisible,' she said with satisfaction. Since they often played inscrutable games together, he thought no more about it but smiled and kissed her before he went away. She drew the shawl around her shoulders and set her feet on the ground. It is hard to say if she actually thought she was invisible; at least, she felt as if she might be. She picked her way delicately towards the window, drew aside the curtain and pressed her face against the cool glass. She saw, in the most immediate, domestic terms, a recreation of the sun and moon in appalling harmony.

Carolyn had become so obsessed with Lee that she had lost all sense of discretion or any sense at all. The landlord had replaced the rusted wrought iron of the lower part of the balcony by some graceless wooden boards so they were concealed from the street but Annabel gazed through the window at them like an infatuated spectre. The spectacle was as silent as if it took place under water and the arrangement of interlocking lines was familiar enough in itself; but this girl's face was vividly contorted, not bland and impassive like that of the whore in the photograph and Lee was lost to her in a secret, ultimate privacy. She could not incorporate this manifestation of his absolute otherness anywhere into her mythology, which was an entirely egocentric universe, and she felt a grieving jealousy of the act itself, which she understood only in symbolic terms.

'If you deceive me, I'll die,' repeated Annabel as if it were a logical formula. If she felt relief and even pleasure each time she herself evaded real contact with him, knowing the magic castle of herself remained unstormed, she thought perhaps he kept the key to the castle, anyway, and one day he might turn against it and rebel. But when she saw rebellion in action, she was forced to desperate measures to disarm him for she might, possibly, perhaps, hopefully, be able by these means to turn an event that threatened to disrupt her self-centred structure into a fruitful extension of it. She let the curtain fall back into place and turned from the window. The party went on as if nothing had happened and Buzz was deep in conversation with a Black man in dark glasses so she could get no help from him. It was practical help rather than comfort she wanted. Because she went stealing with Buzz and they shared the secret of the ring, she did not regard Buzz as too much separate from herself but it was Lee she loved and Lee she now intended to wound.

She went immediately to the bathroom to kill herself in private. Fortunately it was unoccupied. After she locked the door, she remembered she should have borrowed one of Buzz's knives and stabbed herself through the heart. She was irritated to realize she would have to make do with an undignified razor blade but quickly cut open both her wrists with two clean, sweeping blows and sat down on the floor, waiting to bleed to death. She had always bled very easily. She guessed, however, it would take some time to bleed to death. Her wrists ached but she was as content as if she had won another game of chess by unorthodox means.

'They've locked us out,' said Lee.

Carolyn pulled the white dress around her shoulders and laughed.

'I'm absolutely filthy,' she said luxuriously. To be discovered locked out with him in a state of erotic disarray was as public an announcement of their liaison as she could wish and she thought how simple things would now become, a face-to-face confrontation between the Wife and the Other Woman, a certain victory. She wound her arms round him as he tapped at the pane until a blonde girl let them in. Carolyn was too preoccupied with the management of her satin skirts to take any notice of this amazing young woman, whose sullen face, round and white as a saucer of milk, seemed to float in an enormous cloud of peroxide hair, and Lee was too sunk in thought to recognize her until she said: 'Good evening, Mr Collins,' giggled and added, 'sir.'

She was dressed as an incipient tart in a tight, white poloneck sweater, stretch denim trousers and high-heeled boots; only her fat, pale, discontented lips and the startling fairness of her skin hinted at how young she was, the beauty queen of the evening paper, Lee's pupil, to whom he taught current affairs and who now discovered him in a compromising position amidst scenes of drunkenness and drugged debauch.

'Dear God, who brought you, Joanne?'

'Don't worry,' she said. 'I won't breathe a word.'

So he was trapped into complicity with a schoolgirl. Carolyn, looking round, was disappointed to see none of her friends left in the room. Even Buzz had vanished, although the music still played. Lee became edgy and nervous.

'I'll take you home.'

She found her fur wrap on Buzz's cot, beneath some offensive pictures of Lee and Annabel. They left the remains of the party and, as at their first meeting, walked through the quiet streets together as if alone in the world. Suddenly she emitted a rich, low chuckle and pressed his hand but he was by now quite sober and in a state of great agitation for he had behaved more foolishly than he would ever have believed possible.

'The last time my mother communicated to anyone, it was to say she knew she was the Whore of Babylon,' he said, but he was thinking mainly about Annabel. Carolyn turned wide eyes to him; he had never mentioned his mother to her before and she thought this must be the beginning of a further stage of intimacy.

'Tell me about your mother,' she said encouragingly.

'She's locked up,' said Lee. 'Certified.'

She had not expected him to sound so bored.

'Poor Lee,' she said tentatively.

'We was better off with the aunt, wasn't we. You don't want to live with a mad woman, do you, not at the impressionable age.'

A few days later, Buzz showed him the pictures he had taken on the hill. He could never have imagined such terror in her face for he had little capacity for metaphysical dread himself; otherwise, he had foreseen exactly how she would look for the woman in the playground and the girl on the hill were already superimposed on one another in his mind so that to speak of his mother was to speak of Annabel. He noticed his grammar-school accent had given way entirely so he knew he was under stress. Besides, his eyes burned.

'Your aunt . . . your aunt brought you up?'

'Yes. Both of us. She —'

He could not finish the sentence and left it hanging in the air. Carolyn grew sad and a little apprehensive to find no increase but a diminution of intimacy, for he had suddenly become unresponsive to her and she shivered, sensing, perhaps, the imminent loss of a little of her marvellous assurance. She lived in a terrace built out on a cliff over a river, a silent place.

'Are you coming in?'

He gave her a curious look of mild reproof and she felt a premonition of sorrow.

'Lee?'

She stood and beseeched him in the cold midnight in her pretty, silly clothes. But Lee knew he walked some kind of tightrope above a whirlpool, though he believed that the knowledge itself might be enough to avert a fall if he walked carefully and, even if he now intended to break with Carolyn, he was sufficiently sentimental or else, perhaps, vain enough to go upstairs with her. But her room made him vertiginous and he had to keep from the window in case he jumped out. Then he knew he could no longer live at everyday altitudes and had been deceiving himself. He succumbed to guilt immediately.

'What have I done wrong?' she asked like a miserable child, confronted with an indifference which flowed with the magic speed of a Japanese water flower, and now Lee oscillated sickly between two focuses of guilt, his mistress and his wife. Yet all he had wanted from Carolyn, in the first place, had been a little, simple affection and she, from him, pleasure, although now she was in such a tranced and helpless state she thought she would be lonely without him for the rest of her life.

'I don't know you,' said Lee. 'I don't know you at all, do I?'

It was an excuse or an attempt at an explanation rather than a complaint but she was cut to the heart for she did not realize they had only intersected by chance upon one another and exchanged spurious, self-contradictory falsehoods as if flashing lights in one another's faces.

Lee saw the ambulance from the top of the street and broke into a run. He was in time to see them carry Annabel from the house, wrapped in a blanket, and then Buzz spat at him. Buzz was still painted like a fiend and fixed at last upon a situation which fired all his histrionic opportunism.

'I broke the door down and you was off screwing and she dying, wasn't she?'

Lee felt nothing but surprise. Perhaps one of the ambulance men held Lee off him; anyway, soon he found himself in the casualty ward of the hospital giving Annabel's name and address to a nurse. He spelled the name 'Annabel' twice out loud and then found he could not stop repeating the letters unless he kept his hand in front of his mouth. Annabel was nowhere to be seen. A man whose face had been smashed by a bottle lay on a bench, swearing. A pale child inserted sixpence in a machine and withdrew a paper cup of coffee. Another nurse (though perhaps it was one of the first two or one of the onlookers or, indeed, another nurse altogether) offered Buzz a sedative. Lee continued to feel nothing but shock. Annabel on a stretcher, covered up with blankets, vanished through a pair of swing doors. Somebody was trying to inject Buzz with something. What was the child doing here; she could be no more than twelve years old, sitting on a bench, swinging her legs and giggling. Admitted to a night ward without flowers, Annabel would wake in the worst of fears and think herself still dead, if she woke at all, that is.

Once out in the hospital yard, bundled outside by who knew how many nurses, orderlies and extras, Buzz attacked his brother again but Lee broke free and ran for it. The hospital was perhaps a mile and a half away from the quarter where they lived and Lee made his way up the hill by short cuts and back alleys, glancing behind him from time to time, but he soon shook Buzz off and at last found himself in front of Carolyn's house as a church tower somewhere in the city below struck three. He rang Carolyn's bell and she opened the door. Her tawny hair hung down the back of a crimson satin kimono but the yellow light of the street lamps took all her colours away. She saw such misery in his face she grew breathless for she had lain on her narrow bed all the time since he had left her, staring into the darkness, imagining him beside her.

'I knew you'd come back,' she said. 'I just knew.'

'Oh, my love, it's not that,' he said, ashamed. 'Let me in for a while, I can't go home.'

'What's the matter?'

'It's very melodramatic,' said Lee. 'You would hardly believe it.'

They went up the stairs to her room and the lights switched off automatically behind them. Once inside her door, she was startled to see him so grotesquely smeared with Buzz's greasepaint and filthy from the chase through the streets. He dropped his jacket on the floor and lay down on her bed. She did not know what to do and moved about her room uneasily; she was not dressed properly for receiving bad news. Lee found and lit a cigarette, unpleasantly aware that everything he did or said could not fail to breathe stale cliché for he had seen so many scenes of this nature in 'B' feature films, it seemed, in reality, second hand. How was he, then, to invest the horrifying with dignity?

'She . . .'

'Pardon?' she said.

'She tried to end it all, love, she almost did it. My Annabel, that is, Annabel to whom I'm married, that is.'

She lay down beside him and he stroked her hair. She had no vocabulary to deal with the event, either; besides, she had thought of herself only as the Other Woman, never as a Femme Fatale. 'Good heavens,' she thought. 'I must be dangerous.'

'Can I sleep here? I want to keep away from my brother, he's in a homicidal mood.'

'Yes. Of course.' She found she was crying a little and thought Lee must also be crying when it was only the scalding of his hypocritical eyes. As soon as they were in bed together, he did something he could never afterwards explain away or justify to himself; he performed an act which was, in the strictest sense, gratuitous. Because she was female, naked and available, he fucked her while she continued to cry, aware of some gross impropriety but quite unable to resist it. He appeared to be behaving in a perfectly involuntary way, as if to prove to himself he was indeed a villain untouched by any normal human sentiments, and thus extracted from himself a false confession to convince himself, in retrospect, he was immoral although, at the time, he was not thinking of anything at all. Then he fell into a profound sleep from which he was awakened by the insistent ringing of a bell.

'It's the post, I expect,' she said. 'I won't be a minute.'

He could scarcely tear his eyes open but he felt the inrush of cold air into the bed when she left it and heard the rustle of her kimono and the pad, pad, pad of her bare feet. His reactions were extremely slow and he did not say: 'Don't go, it's my brother,' until she had left the room. After a moment, he heard her scream.

The light of early morning flooded the hallway for the front door was wide open and Carolyn leaned against the porch cupping her face in her hands. Blood poured through the cracks between her fingers. Buzz, oddly shamefaced, stood on the doorstep with his hands dangling loosely by his sides, and though he carried his camera, he had not taken any pictures.

'I hit her,' he said. 'I think I broke her nose.'

'We'll have to take her to hospital,' said Lee and began to laugh.

'If you had come down first, I would have killed you.' Buzz showed the knife he held in readiness. He regained a little of his eldritch composure as he did so, cloaked, dark, menacing and fully armed. All the tenants of the rooms in the house peered from their individual doorways to witness the amazing scene and Lee was suddenly exasperated.

'Ah, come off it,' he said. At that, Buzz flung the knife down at his foot as in the old game of daring-with-a-knife they used to play at primary school. The knife stuck quivering in the wooden door jamb. Lee, stark naked, turned and offered to the spies on the staircase the appalling brilliance of his most artificial smile before he pulled out the knife, offered the hilt back to Buzz and shut the front door on him. Carolyn, bleeding profusely, preceded him back up the stairs.

'Please don't call the police, it's a family matter,' said Lee to a woman in a dressing gown.

Carolyn jumped when he touched her but dressed herself and he went to telephone a taxi. He took her into the casualty ward and they attended to her at once. The wounded man and the child had gone but the nurses were the same as before.

'I see you left your brother behind this time,' said the sister, folding her white lips sternly. She was an austere, grey woman of about fifty.

'Annabel,' he said. 'Please?'

'Your private morals are nothing to do with me,' said the sister.

'What the fuck do you mean?' demanded Lee. 'Let me see my wife, won't you?'

'She's awake,' said the sister. 'I must say,' she added with distaste, 'you do have a high casualty rate among your women-folk, don't you?'

Her slight Scots accent lent a steely precision to her speech.

'Tell me about Annabel. I'm legally married to Annabel; doesn't that give me any rights?'

'She had a little breakfast; a boiled egg, toast.'

'Can I see her?'

'She refuses to see you,' the sister replied with an air of grim satisfaction.

Lee sank down on the bench where the bottled man had lain.

'Point-blank?'

'She threatens worse if you persist in trying to see her.'

'I see,' said Lee heavily.

'We're going to move her to a very pleasant psychiatric hospital as soon as it's possible, Mr Collins. You must realize your wife is a very disturbed girl, very sick. Your wife is a girl in need of care, of loving care . . .'

Lee knew the woman judged him and found him wanting and this seemed only fair and just. The nurse reminded him of his aunt, who would have forgiven no act which seemed to her immoral. At that, Lee was convulsed by the knowledge of sin and guilt. Nothing in his education had prepared him for such ravagement and he could guess at no absolution. Besides, his aunt would have mocked the notion for to forgive is only to obliterate and what good does that do?

A changed girl, Carolyn came out through a pair of swing doors. Her reddish brown hair was caked and spiked with dried blood and a muzzle of bandages obscured her pretty face completely. She would not look Lee in the eye and hardly spoke to him as she brusquely brushed past him towards the open air. It was now about eight o'clock on a Sunday morning. Lee had nowhere to go but back to the flat and nothing to do there but clean the bathroom of blood before the rest of the residents in the house, who all shared the bathroom, discovered it had become an abattoir overnight. His clothes were spattered with

Carolyn's blood, also, and soon he saw himself as a red-handed butcher to whom both women seemed no more than curious meat. He had no equipment to deal with abnormal states of mind and his composure utterly deserted him. He entered a delirious state of wilful self-abandonment.

When Annabel found she remained alive, she did not know, at first, how to reconcile herself to it until she hit upon the device of believing herself invisible as long as she wore the skull ring, though she constantly wondered why, if this were so, so many people seemed to be able to see her. This question absorbed her completely and she did not rest in her mind until she found an answer which satisfied her.

'How do you see me?' she asked Buzz. He picked at his lower lip with his fingernail for a while and then replied: 'In fits and starts.'

'That's not good enough,' she said ominously and relapsed into speculation.

'Mrs Collins still refuses to see you,' another sister told Lee, whose home was now unbearable for the tap dripped Annabel's tears and the very sofa seemed re-upholstered with her anguish. At last Buzz led him by the hand to an interview with Annabel's psychiatrist for by now Lee was unable to negotiate the city on his own and could not see where he was going. To compound his distress, he had been drinking heavily during the past fortnight and afterwards he could remember nothing between leaving his house and arriving as if miraculously translated into the warm interior of a cosy hospital with hardly a movement at all on his own part. Buzz abandoned his brother in a room full of faded chintz and old magazines where he waited forty minutes, staring vacantly at an empty wall; intermittently he saw the face of his mother as it had looked after she had been dipped in the petrifying well of madness. Then a nurse came and showed him up a linoleum staircase which shone as if it had been gilded and Lee felt sure it reached almost as high up to heaven as Jacob's ladder although he turned off, as instructed, at the first landing and entered the whitest of offices. Here, he found a young woman seated behind an impressive desk. She was dressed entirely in black and lavishly hung about with hair of metallic yellow. Her eyes were concealed behind tinted glasses and her voice was as if smoked also, dark-toned and husky.

'Mr Collins?'

'Well, yes and no,' replied Lee who always spoke the truth. A look of curiosity passed across her face. She gestured him to sit down.

'A regulation chair of tubular steel,' observed Lee and slithered from it to the ground. Where he lay, he saw how the walls of the room converged upon him from all four corners and crawled for refuge under the desk itself, where he found himself confronted by the woman's high, brown boots in such an unnatural perspective that the feet were enormous and the uppers soared above him like mill chimneys. The boots were so beautifully polished they appeared irradiated from within.

'A kind of expressionist effect,' he said.

'Pardon?'

'Everything is subtly out of alignment. Shadows fall awry and light no longer issues from expected sources.'

'Do you go to the cinema often?'

'Now and then. It stops us all from having to talk to one another though she never follows the story, she only looks at the pictures.'

Since she wore no stockings, the grain of skin appeared to simulate the leather; he stroked her knee and, meeting with no response either in the negative or the affirmative, he explored the outer thigh and then the inner thigh until at last his fingers sank into the hot, wet, hairy cleft itself. At the moment of intimate contact, he experienced a sudden, violent explosion inside his head and instantly re-lived the night of the catastrophe in its entirety.

When the debris cleared, he found himself sprawling on the floor at the other side of the room. He did not know whether the psychiatrist had kicked him away; if he had jack-knifed backwards of his own accord; or whether the whole encounter had taken place only inside his head. He raised himself to his feet and sidled back towards the desk. She sat exactly as she had done before, with her hands laid flat down before her on top of the desk and her face inscrutable.

'Why do you hide your eyes?'

'Photophobia,' she replied. 'Please sit down, Mr Collins.'

Lee did so. He shook his head to try and clear it.

'Here . . . did I touch you up just now?'

The woman laughed and laughed. 'What can you have been using?'

'What?'

'What drug? What drug have you been using?'

'Ethyl alcohol.'

'Besides that.'

'He forces a fistful down me in the morning and another fistful at night. They're very colourful.'

'What are?'

'The pills.'

'He?' enquired the woman.

'My brother.'

'Your brother's visits cause some distraction in the ward. A schizophrenic immediately identified him with St John the Baptist.'

'Our mum thought he was the Anti-Christ. She's mad, too.'

'Is that so?' said the woman with a glimmer of interest.

'Yes, but she went mad on purpose.' Arbitrarily he decided to give her his dazzling smile.

'Do that again!' she said instantly. Lee put up his hands to his face, startled and ashamed.

'How would you describe your relations with your wife? Are they good or bad?'

'Neither good nor bad. They exist. She's been ill before.'

'Ill?'

'Mad, then,' said Lee. Tears fell down his cheeks.

'Such mercurial changes of mood!' observed the woman. 'Why are you crying?'

'Photophobia.'

She switched the light off so that shadows of approaching dusk filled the room.

'She had a breakdown before I met her. I don't know much about it. I think she tried to kill herself then, too.'

'Do you think you know much about your wife?'

'She's a silly cow.'

'Do you think you understand her?'

'No.'

'Why do you think she refuses to see you?'

'She's mad.'

'Apart from that.'

'She believes in keeping herself to herself.'

'Try again.'

'Didn't she tell you why?'

'She doesn't say much. She only plays with the ring on her finger and sometimes she smiles.'

'Her wedding ring, is it?'

'No, not her wedding ring. She ate her wedding ring.'

'Ate it?' repeated Lee incredulously.

'When nobody was looking, yes.'

'Then how do you know she really ate it, if nobody was looking.'

'She told me she ate it with a good deal of conviction. And it was nowhere to be seen. And she smiled; rather a smug smile, I thought.'

'She must have seen me at it, then.'

'At what?'

'I was on the balcony, knocking off this chick, wasn't I.'

57

'The night of the suicide attempt?'

Lee nodded.

'Apart from that, was it a normal evening?'

'There was a party.'

'During which you copulated upon a balcony.'

There followed a silence. After a while, she asked him: 'Do you love your wife?'

'Is there a kind of litmus paper you could dip into my heart and test such a thing objectively?'

'So you feel no affection for your wife.'

'Don't be facile,' said Lee, irritated.

'Why were you having intercourse with this young woman on this balcony?'

'I was drunk.'

'I would have assumed you were drunk,' she said with some asperity. 'But did you act on the spur of the moment or was she an old friend?'

The room seemed so dark to Lee he could hardly make out the colour of the woman's hair though he could see perfectly well that, outside the window, the sky was still light.

'I'd been sleeping with Carolyn, her name is Carolyn – I'd been sleeping with Carolyn for some little time owing to thinking it would ease the strain.'

'Did your relations with this girl alter your behaviour to your wife?'

'Oh, yes. I was much nicer to her.'

'I see,' said the woman in a satisfied voice, as though she had expected him to say this. 'Do you feel guilty?'

'Rather guilty,' said Lee and gave her his dazzling smile, secure she could not see it because it was so dark. Then they were silent again until Lee said, as if to himself:

'Sometimes she hardly seems alive at all, at the best of times. Annabel, she's like a shadow that sits and remembers and probably the things it remembers never happened.'

'It . . .' said the woman reflectively. 'How odd you should refer to your wife as "it".'

'I was referring to the shadow of my wife.'

'I see,' she said and made a note on her pad. 'What is the nature of both your relationships with your brother?'

'Complex.'

'Your brother does not seem to be entirely normal,' she said gently.

'In our milieu, that's something of a compliment, you bourgeois cow.'

'Has it come to personal abuse already?' she enquired pleasantly.

'Abuse or violence, take your choice. But if you took your boots off, I'd kiss your insteps with pleasure.'

'I'm sure you would,' she replied in a comfortable voice. 'Your brother seems to take your wife's fantasies for granted, as if they were real.'

'Maybe.'

'How do you yourself regard your wife's fantasies?'

'I dunno. What a question. I don't know from one minute to the next what it is that exists for her, it's like a flicker book.'

'Does your wife want children?'

'Sweet Jesus!' said Lee, aghast.

'Have you ever discussed having children with her?'

'No. No, I've hardly thought about it beyond the odd scare now and then. Why do you ask? Would you think it was normal?'

'In many circles,' she said. 'Now you've started to cry again, I can hear you.'

'I told you, I have bad eyes.'

'But the lights are all out. How can your photophobia affect you? You have no excuse for tears except sentimentality.'

'Then turn the lights on again, save me my face.'

She did so. She was more black and gold than ever, like a holy image in a very white case and her veiled regard, half-hidden by smoked glass, gave her face an oracular ambiguity so that her blunt-lipped mouth, which might have brought forth snakes, issued slow words with a pregnant weight although now she produced a mere banality.

'Perhaps Annabel should get a job and try to make friends of her own outside the environment imposed on her by yourself and your brother.'

'What's that again?' gasped Lee, stunned; he had been anticipating something portentous.

She said: 'I don't think your brother is a suitable person to live in the same house as such an unbalanced girl as Annabel. Indeed, it is probably very bad for them both.'

'Dear God, do I have to choose between them?'

'There is a condition of shared or, rather, mutually stimulated psychotic disorder known as "*folie à deux*". Your brother and your wife would appear excellent candidates for it. Will you please stop crying. You are beginning to embarrass me.'

'I told you, I can't help it. Here, have I really got to cope with her on my own?'

She shrugged enigmatically.

'What's wrong with my brother?' he demanded truculently.

She threw back her golden head and laughed for a long time until Lee reluctantly began to laugh also for he knew very well what she meant.

'Listen,' he said through his laughter. 'I feel very bad at the moment and I'll tell you why, if you can't guess. I've a brother who tried to kill me and a wife who tried to kill herself and I was searching, you know? For the causal link and so I found myself.'

'Pardon?'

'I'm the plus, aren't I?'

'The plus?'

'One plus one equals two but first we must define the nature of "plus". They have a world which they have made so they can understand it and it includes me at the centre; somehow I am essential to it, so that it can go on. But I don't know anything about it or what I'm supposed to do except be bland and indefinable, like the Holy Spirit, and see the rent gets paid and the bloody gas bill and so forth.'

'It's a hermetic world, the three of you. Will it really admit nobody else?'

'I tried, didn't I. And look what happened then.'

'Well,' she said. 'I'm not concerned with your brother, he isn't a patient of mine. My, but you really are crying.'

'I am the Spartan boy but no fox under my jacket, only my heart, eating itself out.'

'How self-indulgent you are!'

'It's not so much that. It's more that I've lost my capacity for detachment. I lost it on that memorable night. And I used to be so proud of it, as well, joking about her nightmares and so on.'

With that, he gave her the evil, twisted grin he had always kept only for his own amusement in the past and saw how it offended her so much she immediately ceased to be his friend. Whatever sexual or sympathetic undercurrent in this parody of an interview that had contrived to maintain it for so long now vanished. She became brisk and officious. She was clearly about to send him away with an implicit reprimand.

'Think of it this way. There is a sick girl who needs care and can turn only to you. Dry your eyes and look out of the window.'

He saw a green park where lay a lake surrounded by weeping willows whose leafless branches trailed in the motionless water. Dusk was falling but slow figures well muffled against the cold still interminably walked these melancholy grounds and Lee thought he had never seen so many people all together who seemed, each one, so entirely alone. Annabel sat on a bench beside the lake, gazing at its surface which was as black as if of some impermeable substance and not liquid at all. Around her, the silent crowd came and went, absorbed in a multitude of reflections. Since Annabel wore the skull ring on her finger, she could see but not be seen. No flicker of the nerves of her face indicated she watched him approach but suddenly she drew the ring off and threw it away. The waters closed over it and concentric ripples spread out without a sound over the place where it sank. Never before had she felt the extent of her powers until that moment, when she resolved to be visible all the time and was rewarded by seeing him drawn towards her whether he willed it or not, as if she were a magnetic stone.

'I love you,' she said.

She spoke in sweet, fallacious music like the song of a mechanical nightingale and now she seemed to him a ghostly woman, white as a winding-sheet and shrouded in hair. The darkening light seemed to pass straight through her almost dissolving edges and when she stretched out her hands towards him they looked like dried flowers, nothing but veins and transparency, and he could see the bones of her fingers through them. The sky was serene and no wind nor flight of any bird moved in the leafless branches of the trees or stirred the still air of winter.

Lee took Annabel in his arms and she buried her face in his breast but he could not forbear to look behind him, towards the hospital buildings. Silhouetted against a bright window, the psychiatrist watched them through her dark glasses. The light behind her illuminated her flamboyant hair so she seemed all of a piece with the brightness itself and as she raised her arm either in a kind of blessing or, more likely, to draw the blinds as if dismissing all her patients for the night, she seemed to Lee like some kind of inexorable angel, directing him to where his duty lay.

'Do right because it is right,' said Lee.

Lazzaro Spallanzani observed division in bacteria; his bladder is preserved in the museum at Pavia, in Italy. Pursuing his biological studies, Spallanzani cut off the legs of a male toad in the midst of its copulation but the dying animal did not relax the blind grasp to which nature drove it. Spallanzani therefore concluded: 'The persistence of the toad is due less to his obtuseness of feeling than to the vehemence of his passion.'

Like Spallanzani's toad, Lee was not insensitive to his situation but the stern puritanical fervour of his childhood condemned him, now, to abandon himself to the proliferating fantasies of the pale girl whose arms clasped as tight around his neck as if she were drowning. He might have guessed her history would be brief and tragic for she had always worn the blind face of those who will die young and so do not need to see much of life; but the moral imperative, to love her, proved stronger than his perceptions and his natural desire for happiness persuaded him, at first, that his intuitive forebodings were unjustified.

Besides, he was full of guilt.

Now Lee knew they would not let Annabel come home until his brother was expelled from the household, he saw Buzz as if he had never known him. He watched the variously obsessed figure intently. It continued to go busily about the absurd tasks it set itself as if they were perfectly natural. It sharpened its knives; it splashed in its acids; it snipped, stitched and dyed its commedia dell'arte rags; it rolled its joints with a pompous ritual worthy of a sacrament; it squatted for hours on the floor in those hollow, interminable silences with which it passed its excess wastes of useless time, and Lee saw all this as the motions of an unfamiliar object. He marvelled that he could have endured its aberrations so long and began to harden against the thing he saw. Until this time, he had scarcely differentiated between his brother and himself; Buzz was a necessary attribute, an inevitable condition of life. But now the circumstances were altered. Annabel freshly defined Lee as having no life beyond that of a necessary attribute of herself alone, and, in this new arrangement, Lee knew his brother for an interloper who might do harm. So now a cancer lodged at the core of his heart, where Buzz had been. Besides, he found the pictures which Buzz had taken of Annabel in the bathroom, before he called the ambulance.

Once the process of dissociation began, it quickly gathered impetus. He felt a sharp distaste at the close physical contact which had been bred of their extreme intimacy. If, at first, he believed he felt a new distaste rather than a positive revulsion, he could no longer drink from a cup Buzz had used unless he rinsed it out and the casual embraces they had always exchanged so thoughtlessly became intolerable for him. Their affection dissipated with extraordinary speed for, had they not been brothers, they would have had little in common and they could not maintain between them an uncommitted state of mutual forbearance without the sustenance of love. Buzz was helpless, incredulous and a little fearful as he perceived the growth of Lee's aversion and strove to protect himself from pain by jeers, by coldness and by the pretence of disdain. He schooled himself in dislike and waited for the blow to fall.

Lee expected a display of panic and violence when he told Buzz he would have to leave the flat but Buzz, well prepared, showed no anger or surprise. He continued to sit before the fire in perfect silence, drumming his fingers on his knee, while Lee wondered nervously what the unguessable response might be. But, when it came, it was scrupulously cool.

'Going straight?' asked Buzz in a normal voice, though with a touch of contempt.

Lee shrugged. They did not look at one another. Time passed. Coals fell in the grate. It was night-time.

'Where shall I live?' said Buzz.

'We'll find somewhere for you easily,' said Lee with false cheerfulness.

'When shall I move out?'

'As soon as you can find a place.'

'And will you let me come to see you, now and then?'

'Sure,' said Lee, touched and embarrassed. 'Of course.'

'Sure,' repeated Buzz equivocally. He recommenced drumming his fingers and Lee's embarrassment and distress grew with every moment that passed for, if he could brave out his brother's wildest passions, this unaccountable quiet nonplussed him and he feared it might be the prelude to some absolutely unexpected act against which he had no defence. Downstairs, another occupant of the house began to run a bath and the sound of running water drifted upstairs.

'Lee . . . who shall I talk to?'

'It's not that you talk to me, much.'

'But you're always there. And she, there's always Annabel to talk to.'

'I'm not divorcing you, for God's sake. We'll still be here, both of us.'

'You'll ask me to dinner once a month, perhaps, will you?'

Lee realized his brother's attack was cunningly directed at his sentimentality and began to lose his temper. The fantastic room became abhorrent and the dark figure who sat on the carpet took on the aspect of a giant, hairy toad squatting upon his life and choking him, since this obscure being was a more fitting inhabitant of the room than himself. Yet the room belonged to Annabel; she had painted her ambivalent garden on the walls and installed Lee in the midst of it whether he matched her colours or not. Lee broke out in confused fury.

'She's mine.'

'Is she?' said Buzz in sardonic enquiry, turning his hard, brown gaze upon his brother. At this precise moment in time, Lee ceased to love him. The few remaining bonds snapped altogether and at once as they knelt before the fire and bickered about the girl who, like a Victorian heroine, had come between them. Yet Lee still had not the faintest idea what he could do with her once he got her to himself or how he might make some reparation to her, in order to relieve his guilt. He might, perhaps, clean out her room and throw her things away for he half believed her some malleable substance on whom the one who rescued her from her phantoms could impose whatever form he pleased.

Since he was racked with pity for her, he chose to try to rescue her for fear of what she might become if she were left to herself or to the unscrupulous mercies of another, for he did not know she had plans of her own and would finally choose to attempt to save herself.

'Mine,' repeated Lee and, rising, swept the mantelpiece clear of all its assorted rubbish with a sweep of his arm. The rubbish fell down around the fireplace; the skull of the horse shattered in shards of bone and the pottery Prince Albert snapped in two at the waist. Buzz continued to look at him with those opaque eyes which were, in no sense, the mirrors of his soul. He offensively took out and lit a cigarette.

'Turning me out of our home,' he said. 'What would our auntie think?'

Lee's heart contracted and he would have lashed out if Buzz had not been his brother.

'No point in consulting the dead,' he said with an attempt at calm.

Buzz threw his cigarette into the fire and kicked the coals with his booted foot. As he rose, he towered above Lee. His coat of long-haired fur took on the appearance of scalps, his hair shook out like that of a brave and his endless, emaciated shadow flickered across the ceiling as if the shadow of his influence dominated the room. His appearance was so fearful that Lee braced himself for the shock of impact or even the cut of a knife but he received only a mouthful of empty threats, as he would have expected in the old days before he lost his detachment.

'Do anything to her like you did last time and I'll get you, I really will.'

'You're too bloody inefficient,' snarled Lee, freshly infuriated at this dramatic flourish, but Buzz was out through the door before the shaft struck home and when Lee came back from work next day, he found not one of his brother's possessions remained in the flat. Every last rag and scrap of paper was gone and he had not left a note of acrimonious farewell or the gift of his new address which might have hinted at the possibility of a reconciliation. Only a few blotches on the floor showed he had ever lived there. His dark room echoed to Lee's footsteps with a hollow sound.

He took a suitcase for her things to the psychiatric hospital and, now he was in full possession of his faculties, the building struck him by the witty irrelevance of its grandeur to its purpose.

One approached it through wrought-iron gates; a double drive swept round on each side of a defunct fountain in the form of a triton who raised up a scallop shell to spill no water any more, only a stain of rust into the marble basin below. On either side of the building stretched pleasant lawns and formal beds of standard rose trees on which a few withered blooms still languished. He saw the lake where he had found Annabel was not a lake at all, only a lily pond in the shape of a tear. All served as a decorative prelude to a harmonious Palladian mansion whose present use was indicated only by a discreet notice board, half hidden in a privet hedge. A young boy in a long dressing gown and several mufflers who lurked on the porch glared mutinously at Lee as he ascended the wide, gleaming, marble steps to the front door.

'This house was built in the Age of Reason but now it has become a Fool's Tower,' said the boy. 'Are you familiar with the tarot pack?'

Lee with his suitcase was so intimidated by the mansion that he felt like a travelling salesman and could only smile and nod ingratiatingly for he was eloping with the duke's daughter; but when she saw him, she grasped his hand with a strangely passionate pressure and suddenly kissed him. He scanned her face for signs of change but her pale, haunted composure was that of the morning he first woke to see her. He glanced down at her bare hands.

'I'll buy you a new ring,' he said.

'One with a moonstone?'

'Maybe,' he replied, with a sense of foreboding.

'I'd rather spend the money on something else,' she said with the air of a child with a secret plan.

'On what?'

'First of all, on a taxi.'

He did not hear her instructions to the driver and found himself unexpectedly in the dockland among mean, steep, cramped streets and low, dark shops. Annabel's features grew unusually animated; she glanced at him from time to time with a repressed, anticipatory glee. From the window, Lee saw a gaunt figure emerge from a doorway folded in the wings of a black cape like Poe's raven named Nevermore but the taxi turned a corner and Buzz, if Buzz it were, was gone. The taxi deposited them on a main thoroughfare by a shop window above which a sign read: ARTIST IN FLESH.

The window was full of coloured photographs demonstrating the full range of the art of the tattooist. Men turned into artificial peacocks displayed chests where ramped ferocious lions, tigers or voluptuous houris in all the coloured inks which issued from the needle. One man had the head of Christ crowned with thorns in the centre of his bosom and another was striped all over like a zebra. Some had flowers, memorial crosses and the words: MOTHER R.I.P. A young girl coyly raised her skirt to show a flock of butterflies tattooed along her thigh. In the centre of the window hung a very large photograph of a man upon whose entire back was described a writhing dragon in reds and blues; and every scale and fang of the beast, each flame it blew from its nostrils, was punctured into the skin for good and all unless he were unpeeled like an orange or pared like an apple. Lee experienced a sympathetic crawling of the flesh; sure, now, of her purpose, he glanced in astonishment at Annabel, who smiled seraphically and pushed at the shop door.

Lee did not know whether this ordeal was a piece of retribution or a rite of passage; nevertheless, he underwent it. The tattooist wore a prim, white, surgical coat and cleansed the ritual of a little barbarism by his care for hygiene, although the clinical asepsis of his shop and the gross attention he paid to the points and sterility of his needles affronted Lee, who could have wished for more atrocious pain, torrents of blood and an ultimate, festering wound to compensate Annabel in full for the skill with which she had devised this baroque humiliation, if she had intended to humiliate him; and, try as he might, he could think of no other reason for the exercise.

Shirtless in an enamel cubicle, he let them write her name indelibly in Gothic script and circle it with a heart so now he wore his heart on the outside, laid bare for all to see. A man in the window had a sacred heart on his left breast and Lee was now equipped with a new heart, also, as if the old one had been cut out, hand-coloured, pressed flat and re-consecrated entirely to Annabel, no longer his own to do with as he pleased. His new, visible heart was drawn in rosy red but, for her name, she chose the colour green. The needle attacked him like an electric bee and he stung and sweated beneath it, biting his lower lip, while she watched the artist plying his tool with intense concentration, her colourless mouth ajar and the tip of her tongue protruding between her teeth. When Lee put his shirt back on, she made him pay and smiled once again, far more radiant than she had been as a bride. Weak and sick, Lee went out with her into the morning and she took his hand in hers, her long, narrow hand which was always nervously moist and unnaturally warm.

'You'll never deceive me again,' she said with pale conviction. 'What other girl would make love to you now?'

Lee realized he had credited her with more emotional sophistication than she possessed. She believed only that she had signed him; the mark was no more than a certificate of possession which gave him the status of any other object in her collection. She had not intended to humiliate him and was hardly capable of devising a revenge which required a knowledge of human feeling to perfect it. Nevertheless, he had been humiliated, even if it were no concern of hers. In wet weather, the tattoo seemed to throb and burn him; in dry weather, it itched intolerably and he was always nervously conscious of her name under his left nipple, shuddering as it did at every beat of his heart. Annabel was very pleased with the effect. Perhaps, he thought, it was a bad-conduct medal.

So they began their life alone together in the knowledge she had won a major victory over him and Lee could no longer pretend that he had rescued her. She sustained her conviction of supremacy so strongly, if in perfect silence, that soon he began to act as if he had indeed been utterly vanquished and let go all the acquaintances he had managed to keep. He ceased to visit anywhere outside the flat and spent all his free time with her. He became as silent and decorative as the statue with which she had always compared him while their home rotted around them, suffused with purgatorial gloom.

She never mentioned Buzz's name and he never came to see them. Lee sometimes thought he would never see his brother again for as long as he lived. He had no desire to see his brother but a visit from him would have proved that the past had existed. And now he had no other evidence that his life could once have been other than the way he lived now. His family photographs were not objective evidence that the beings in them had ever moved in a real, accessible dimension. His guilt had devised its own punishment. He acknowledged that she was far cleverer than he and began to fear her a little for he could not alter her at all, although she could change him in any way she pleased.

And now Annabel had docketed him securely amongst her things, she began subtly to evacuate herself from the room which had been her whole world, leaving Lee marooned there in miserable isolation.

Now she had two rooms, her unseen world extended its physical boundaries, though it seemed she no longer needed to populate it with as many real objects as before, perhaps because she had impressed her sorrow so deeply on the essential wood and brick of the place she knew for certain nobody could ever be happy there again. She no longer exchanged confidences with the figures on the walls. She did not bother to buy any more furniture or even to fill up the mantelpiece with bunches of leaves and berries from the park stuck into the necks of milk bottles. She lay in bed for hours while Lee was at work, sometimes drawing her pet apocalyptic beasts in her sketchbook but, more and more, merely gazing into space, absorbed in thought. The window remained boarded up and the room was always dark and shady.

Some days she did not get up at all and, if she did, she did not bother to dress or wash but lounged around all day in her nightdress, the very image of mad Ophelia, her disordered hair often caked with watercolour or gobbed with breakfast egg. But now she knew who mad people were and how they behaved, she became a little self-conscious and sometimes she looked like a blurred imitation of her former self. She did not take the drugs which had been prescribed for her and flushed them down the lavatory to conceal this omission from Lee. She kept none of her after-care appointments with the psychiatrist, but took good care to dress herself neatly on certain days of the week, as if she were going to the hospital, and Lee believed her.

Accustomed as he was to dealing with the sick, Lee fed her and cared for her, although, in herself, she seemed much the same as she had always been. Besides, he had few patterns of normal behaviour with which to compare and contrast her ways.

One day, she roused herself sufficiently to go downstairs and put his alarm clock in the dustbin. She said that the tick irritated her. After that, there was no more means of telling the time except for Lee's wristwatch, so he was often late for work, although the days he passed at the school were scarcely different from the nights he passed at home. Both were barren. He felt as though all his vitality had drained out through the perforations of the needle. Each morning on the stairs, he passed the blonde girl, Joanne, and the swift, fascinated distaste in her glance instantly defined him as a debauched, shameless and abandoned person. Her look made Lee nervous and a little wistful. But she never missed crossing his path on the staircase and he was always aware of her precociously slumberous gaze fixed on his face when he gave her form their weekly lessons on current affairs and political institutions.

Seated at the round table in the bleak middle of a Sunday afternoon, he marked a pile of fifth-form essays on the British Constitution and found, written in a round, childish hand, only the following words on one sheet of paper: 'They say this is a free country but I am not free in any way so stuff your free country.' It was difficult to mark Joanne's essay or to guess at the impulse which prompted it, though he thought she would not have submitted it to any other member of the staff. He scrawled 'amplify' at the bottom in red but she did not do so; it seemed the written word was not Joanne's medium. She had a name for waywardness but Lee paid no attention to staffroom gossip though he noticed in class she was always biting her nails and her nails were brown with nicotine.

An unhappy adolescent will clutch at any straw. Joanne, who was dissatisfied, incorporated her schoolteacher in her own illusory web where, quite unknown to himself and entirely without his consent, he led a busy, active life of high adventure and almost continuous sexual intercourse. She had never received much real affection. Her mother was dead and her father an alcoholic. When she was a small child, she found a wounded pigeon beside the railway line. Its breast and leg were hurt. She nursed it until it grew better and exercised it by allowing it to fly round and round her room. At first, as it learned once more how to fly, it blundered about from mantelpiece to chest of drawers like a raw beginner, bungling every movement, but soon it gained confidence and swooped around beneath the ceiling with the heavy grace of pigeons. It slept in the bottom of her wardrobe. One night it escaped from her room and fluttered downstairs into the kitchen where it sat on the plate rack of the gas stove, cooing, until the sound irritated her father, who kicked it to death.

She was an enthusiastic competitor in minor beauty contests out of a poignant, though unconscious, desire to be publicly acknowledged a pretty girl, yet she had a certain optimism and thought she might easily satisfy her desires as soon as she was sure what they were.

Lee sank more deeply into a melancholy so alien to his nature it never occurred to him he might be unhappy for he associated unhappiness with a positive state, with scarcely tolerable grief or furious sorrow authenticated by a death or a disaster, not with this unmotivated absence of pleasure that dulled the colours of the approaching spring and took the dimensions from the things around him so everything was reduced to flat, ineffectual

73

shapes. He raised his arm and no shadow fell for Annabel had taken out his heart, his household god, squashed it thin as paper and pinned it back on the exterior, bright, pretty but inanimate.

Yet, always on the point of disintegrating, he contrived somehow always to hold himself together for he sincerely believed that, since the world was so full of a number of things, it was a moral imperative to be happy as a king. This was the final modification of his puritanism; that if he had enough to eat and a roof over his head, he knew he ought to be content even if the king he always thought of in connection with the smiling couplet he repeated to himself every morning was Mad King Ludwig of Bavaria. He lost his self-consciousness for it no longer served him any function and he revealed the aggressive reserve which had always lain beneath his acquired ease of manner. He ceased, almost immediately, to be charming but his beautiful, collected walk changed, or, rather, intensified in character. He strode along with more determination and far greater arrogance now he knew there was nowhere to go.

If his fatal sentimentality demanded that the promises he had made her and the anguish they had shared should, in some way, unite them, he could see with his own eyes that no union had been achieved. Because they spent so much time in silence, it was always possible for Lee to deceive himself they shared an unspoken and profound closeness; only when he occasionally spoke to her did the space between them become apparent and sour. By Easter, he had almost given up talking altogether and smiled only in fits of extreme absence of mind.

Their life passed in a diffused dreariness and Lee could not guess the subject of Annabel's reveries for she took good care not to speak of the absent brother. Besides, she did not suffer from the loss of her playfellow for, since she no longer saw him every day, every day he became more real to her and, though she did not long for him, she waited for his physical return with a certain irritation that it was delayed so long. On the other hand, he might return to her in some other shape. Sometimes she thought of him as a mean, black fox and sometimes as a metamorphic thing that could slip in and out of any form he chose, so surely he could briefly inhabit a bird perching outside on the balcony, for he had no fear of heights. Then, again, he was equally at home in subterranean regions and could have become a mouse she sometimes heard, gnawing the interior of the wall. She remembered the game they had played with his father's ring and thought it very likely he could shift his shape and come to visit her, if only with the other shadows, at night. She grew more friendly with the night-time shapes of things, for now they might possess identities.

Although she hardly budged from her bed, she often, in her turn, visited him in his new room. He had found himself a dark and brooding habitation where light filtered thickly, if at all, through blackened windows on to his piled relics and everywhere among the knives and jars of acid hung photographs of herself. She spent far more time in this imaginary room than she did in her own home, which seemed to her now not a home but a transitory lodging. She threw away Buzz's ring only in order to deceive her husband for she had decided to embark upon a new career of deceit and she knew, if she were clever, she could behave exactly as she wished without censure or reprimand, almost as if she were invisible whether she wore the ring or not. Lee no longer dared be angry with her no matter if she stole, forbore to wash, or pushed him away in bed because he was so frightened of the possible consequences.

When she was two or three years old, her mother took her shopping. Little Annabel slipped out of the grocer's while her mother discussed the price of butter and played in the gutter for a while until she decided to wander into the middle of the road. A car braked, skidded and crashed into a shop front. Annabel watched the slivers of glass flash in the sunshine until a crowd of distraught giants broke upon her head, her mother, the grocer in his white coat, a blonde woman with dark glasses, a man with four arms and legs and two heads, one golden, the other black, and many other passers-by, all as agitated as could be imagined. 'You might have been killed!'

said her mother. 'But I wasn't killed, I was playing,' said Annabel, no bigger than a blade of grass, who had caused this huge commotion all by herself just because she could play games with death.

However, this was not the memory of a real event but of a particularly lifelike dream she had under sedation in the hospital although she now believed it to be perfectly true. In the hospital, she could create confusion by a gesture as simple as gulping down her wedding ring; she learned how uncommon she was and so she acquired an aristocratic sense of privilege and, with it, an aristocratic sense of disdain, for all around her she received hints and intimations that her fantasies might mould the real world. She leafed through the *National Geographic* magazine in the lounge and saw pictures of long-horned steers so she decided to brand Lee like the cattle of the Old West as a first test of her occult powers.

When she abandoned drawing completely, she paradoxically appeared to rouse from her physical lethargy. First, with a kind of abstracted wilfulness, she took to wandering around the streets all day; then, one afternoon, she found what she was seeking, a sign advertising the post of an assistant in the window of a draper's. She went in and was hired on the spot. At first, Lee thought this action was a hopeful sign. Instead, it was the beginning of a period during which she mimicked Buzz's pattern of casual labour in her own fashion.

She drifted haphazardly from one undemanding, unskilled job to another, working sometimes as a waitress, sometimes packing biscuits in a factory before moving on to a fish-and-chip shop or a department store. She seemed to want to try her hand at anything. She earned a little money for herself but she had given up buying things so there was nothing to spend it on. She kept the notes in an Oxo tin bound with an elastic band on the bedroom mantelpiece and, with the small change, she bought chocolate bars, cream cakes, sugar buns and other sweet, unnecessary things she consumed immediately, as if it were pocket money and she were twelve years old. It never occurred to Lee to touch any of her money. It could have turned to dead leaves the moment she put it inside her tin.

He lost his first optimism as he saw she grew no closer to the common world by mingling with it; rather, she enhanced her own awareness of her difference from it and grew proud. He learned to treat her desultory employments with a weary indulgence even if he were always apprehensive about her for he no longer had any notion of how, in a new set of circumstances, she might behave. But Annabel felt a nascent sense of clarification. She had never felt exhilarated before but now she felt herself stirring. It seemed to her that the concealed shapes which had so long menaced her were casting off their ambiguous surfaces and revealing, not the perfect shapes of fear she had so long suspected beneath them, but soft, indeterminate, interior cores. The world unshelled itself or she unshelled the world and she found, beneath the crust of spiked armour, a kernel of plasticine limply begging to be rendered into forms. As she grew more confident this was so, she drew a final picture of Lee as a unicorn whose horn had been amputated. Her imagery was by no means inscrutable. Then her sketchbooks were put away for good.

She longed to share the discoveries she had made with Buzz but she was not impatient to find him again. Her new theory of magic presentiments assured her he would appear again when the time was ripe. She guessed the institution of a new order of things in which she was an active force rather than an object at the mercy of every wind that blew; no longer bewitched, she became herself a witch.

Lee knew nothing of this access of a confidence as strange to him as her former terrors.

As if she was determined, now, to inhabit only incongruous places, her disinterested career in the world took her to work in a local ballroom, one of a chain which operates throughout the provinces. For her duties, she wore a sheath of pink, yellow and white printed cotton slit up to the thigh on the left side and she had to pin a bunch of pink and yellow artificial flowers in her hair. The manager selected a dress he thought might fit her from a folded heap of similar dresses in a musty cupboard and the fabric smelled of disuse and old, stale sweat reawakened by the warmth of her body; it was in no way her own dress and when she looked at herself in the mirror of the changing room she saw, indeed, a stranger. When she was thirteen, she managed to spend a whole year without looking in a mirror for fear of seeing there a different face from her own but, this time, if she felt a passing terror, it was rather at the memory of this old dread than a suspicion it might reassert itself and she shook with excitement for this stranger in vulgar and whimsical clothes who began to smile a little at her, shyly, quite misrepresented herself. This stranger had an appearance not altogether unlike that of ordinary charm.

Annabel pushed her long hair back from her face and practised the smile Lee used to give her in bed, before he gave up smiling. The effect was enchanting and seemed to express utter guileless-ness and a marvellous warmth of heart. So she counterfeited the only spontaneous smile he had and took it away from him, leaving him with no benign expressions left for himself. Equipped with this delicious smile, she entered the ballroom and found a cold, bewitching dazzle of lights. Here, since everything around her was artificial, she and her first, carefully contrived, if tentative, reconstruction of herself as a public object passed for a genuine personality.

Everything in this ballroom was absolutely similar to the interiors of all the other ballrooms in the chain, so it was a synthetic reduplication without an original model and there was nothing in it at all peculiar to itself. The bar where Annabel worked was decorated to represent a grove of palm trees spread-ing green fronds over small, rustic, wooden tables and low stools. The walls were lavishly garnished with fishing nets and, caught in the hanging folds, were brilliantly coloured, luminous, tropic fish, flowers and fruit. Candles placed inside large purple brandy glasses served not to illuminate but to enhance the primary illusion of luxurious darkness. In the swathes of mauve tulle which concealed the ceiling above the dancing floor hung a rotating, many-faceted witchball upon which a spotlight was permanently directed so roving tracks of light scurried about the floor all the time like shining, fleshless mice and concealed lighting effects all round the room caught the dancers in sudden, cold, blue blizzards or washed them with crimson.

Smiling her borrowed smile, a false Eve in an artificial garden, Annabel served drinks and washed out glasses, to all appearances distinguished from the other girls in pink and yellow dresses only by her height and her distinctive slimness. But she still rarely spoke and customers and staff alike treated her with a certain circumspection for she had no notion of how to behave naturally except in the way which was natural to her. She worked in this place for five nights out of the week, from seven o'clock to eleven o'clock on Monday, Tuesday and Wednesday and from seven o'clock to one the next morning on Friday and Saturday. Under these circumstances, she was only infrequently at home when Lee was there. All the time she was away from him, he was afraid for her although he was not sure why and, on the nights she worked very late, he went to the ballroom to bring her home. Then they would take the short cut, through the park. Sometimes, when there was a moon, she would grasp convulsively at his hand but usually she walked quietly beside him while he watched their shadows preceding them along the ragged path like shadows of a nonexistent harmony. One Saturday night, Lee became involved in a fight in the ballroom.

As on the other Saturday nights, she carried her smile through the customers like a person carrying a basin full to the brim with water who has to move very carefully so that not a drop is spilled. Lee arrived at the club before she expected him and she was disconcerted; she hid for a while behind a plastic tree to see what he was like when he was by himself for lately she sometimes wondered if he existed at all when she was not beside him to project her idea of him upon him. His by now a little battered beauty was always at odds with the environment in which he happened to find himself for he still looked more than ever like a handsome outlaw even if he was a schoolteacher by profession, so she was not surprised to see him grow in self-possession in the ballroom, out of self-defence.

Later, watching him closely as she washed glasses behind the bar, she was so sure he was her creature she felt only a little angry contempt and pity when he approached the blonde girl for she could see the fluorescent outlines of his heart and her own name glowing beneath his clothes and knew he could not act independently. By a piece of mental sleight of hand, she rendered the ensuing fight inevitable; she was enchanted by her powers and, laying out the separate events and scrutinizing them as if they were fortune-telling cards, she divined the time was ready for Buzz's return. Soon she might be able to tell the wind when it was time to blow.

Since there was no clock in the house and he had forgotten to wind his watch, Lee relied on intuition as regards the time and so he arrived at the club only a little after midnight for the unmarked hours passed slowly in his silent room. The doorman knew him well by now and allowed him inside to seat himself at a vulgar table and have his wife serve him in surroundings so reminiscent of his working-class origins she looked like an anachronism, anyway. She wore a smile he did not know was a plagiarism since he had never seen himself wearing it; he knew only that it was sweet, unusual and disquieting for it did not seem to belong to her and might hang in the air after she had gone, like that of the Cheshire cat.

Immensely amplified music from an extremely powerful record player and innumerable confusions of coloured lights contended with one another in the air so noisily that, when a man at a nearby table struck a match and held it aloft for a moment before lighting his cigarette, the small, pure, steady flame amidst the clutter of neon was as startling as a chord of silence. The little fire briefly lit up three faces, two of men and one of a girl with a great deal of flaxen hair which sprayed out like flying snow. She was the girl Joanne and at present she was the object of an unpleasant scene of petty sexual bullying. As soon as the match was out, her companion on her right thrust his hand down the opening of her blouse and ostentatiously fondled her right breast. The girl writhed a little in her chair from embarrassment, not from pleasure, and her companion on her left gave a little, mewing giggle and began to fumble with the fastening of her blouse at the back. Both, though still boys, were rather older than she and had a certain elegance of dress and manner; she was clearly a casual pick-up and they could treat her as casually as they pleased.

She was out of her depth and her first signs of fright gratified them. They laughed at one another across the top of her head and the frantic lights momentarily struck a glittering spoor of tears on her round, white cheeks. When Lee leaned heavily on him and said: 'Leave her alone,' the boy laughed up at him with the serene self-confidence of the middle class mixed with a man-to-man invitation to tolerance and his hand continued to agitate the girl's breast until Lee hit him on the mouth, which transformed the laugh into a gape of dismay.

Disengaging himself from Joanne, the other stuttered: 'Here . . . I say . . .' as if in self-parody. Joanne leaped to her feet and knocked over the table so that everything upon it, glasses, ashtray, brandy glass and candle, rolled and smashed everywhere; in the confusion, she vanished and both boys set on Lee at once while the lighted candle set fire to a swathe of tulle.

Saturday night is the right time for a fight and Lee, a retired veteran of fights in similar times and places, found himself entering into the old spirit. It was like diving back into the past; it was simple, elementary and unpremeditated experience. It had nothing to do with the person he had become.

The first pause in the action occurred when he was thrust back into a drift of flame and lurched forward into the arms of a man in a dinner jacket with a fire extinguisher who pushed him to one side with a curse and attacked the conflagration with squirts of foam. Many of the dancers continued to move to the music as if nothing were happening for both fight and fire were localized in a small part of the ballroom but those nearby the focus of the table had all become involved in it. Lee saw the boy who had caressed Joanne crawling blindly through a labyrinth of legs and overturned chairs, bleeding from the mouth, and some other person was kicking the other boy, who lay on the floor. A few women screamed and smoke billowed out of the smouldering hangings. Another man in a dinner jacket threw a bucket of sand, cigarette ends and dried vomit over the head of the first boy. Perhaps the man had mistaken the contents of the bucket for water. The lights, meanwhile, continued through their various changes so that the chaos was washed by all manner of romantic colours. Lee decided the time had come to leave and slipped out unnoticed. He felt ridiculously light of heart for the insignificant rough-house in the ballroom had reminded him of how simple he had once found it to act without thought and pay attention only to his immediate impulses and gratifications.

So the fight, or tussle, was by no means insignificant for, while he took part in it, he quite forgot Annabel and, during the time he had forgotten Annabel, he was happy without even trying to be so. When he was twenty, he would have reprimanded himself for such self-indulgence, for then he had believed that happiness was a quality which resided in its possessor and bore no relation to his environment. But now he was a little older and had learned his theory was difficult, if not impossible, to work out in practice. Had there been sufficient time, he might have thought rather more about the implications of his sudden, unexpected and remarkable attack of happiness and concluded, at last, that he might have to stop loving Annabel in order to keep intact what few fragments of himself he could save. But, as it proved, there was no time at all.

*

The scrabbling at the door announced a visitor, though nobody ever visited them even if, today, Annabel sat on the sofa with the air of someone waiting for something. The scrabbling persisted and, when neither of the occupants of the room spoke, the door handle turned. It was a warm Sunday afternoon in early June and vivacious sunlight broke against the windows only to shatter on a thick rind of dirt so that a dazzle of blurred light suffused the room and bounced back from sparkling particles of mica here and there in the crepe veil of dust which covered everything. All the shoulders of Annabel's collection of bottles were padded with the dust which ridged the picture frames and rose up in clouds from the rarely disturbed plush of chairs and tablecover if, by chance, they were touched. Images could no longer force their way through the grime on the mirror and the lion's-head handles on the sideboard wore soft, gritty deposits in each wooden eyeball and curl of mane. Dust hooded the glass case so thickly you could not see that the stuffed fox inside was now diseased; its muzzle was grey with mould and its hide sprouted with thriving fungi. There was nothing in the room which did not smudge the hand which brushed it, for Lee had not the time nor the heart to clean or tidy anything and Annabel never thought to. The pigments of her landscapes round the green walls were already beginning to fade so faces yellowed, flowers withered and leaves turned brown in a parody of autumn although, outside, glimpsed darkly through clouded glass, the trees in the garden of the square shook out fresh leaf in the bright air of summer. It was as if the spirit of the perverse so thoroughly inhabited the room it could make what difference it chose even to the seasons of the year.

Unsure of his welcome, Buzz edged slyly into the flat, concealing his nervousness by a manner at once sinuous and ramshackle. He narrowed his eyes to peer round furtively to see how things had changed; he saw a room like a nursery abandoned just as the children had left it when they went to school, filthy, full of broken things, the furniture scattered about the floor in a disorderly, careless fashion and dirty clothes spilling out of the bedroom everywhere. He was quite satisfied.

'Hi, Alyosha,' he said to his brother and sat down on the floor against the wall at his old, Euclidian angle. He exchanged one or two thin remarks with his brother who sat at the table marking third-form essays on aspects of current affairs and then he and Annabel began again their endless conversation of silences and allusions as if there had been no real intermission in it. She was unusually lively and laughed a little from time to time but she did not try her new smile on Buzz for she thought he would see through it immediately. She and Buzz began to smoke and the sweet, heavy odour drifted through the motes dancing on the air, mingling harmoniously with the rich smell of old clothes in the room.

It grew so close and hot that Lee pulled off his shirt. Buzz saw the tattoo at once and turned his eyes to Annabel with open admiration in them; they both broke into peals of derisive laughter and Buzz kept glancing at the mark from time to time in amazed mockery. Once, before Lee acknowledged any difference between what he did and how he responded to it, he had witch-doctored Buzz to tranquillity from one of his sporadic attacks of hysteria by locking him securely in his arms, according to the usual practice, down on the floorboards which had then been white and bare, not smothered up with ragged rugs as they were now. Annabel crouched watching by the fire and, when Buzz finally slept, she came and lay down beyond him, stretching out her hands over his shoulders to caress Lee wistfully and, as she did so, she drowned both brothers in cascades of her pre-Raphaelite hair. That was the only time all three spent the night together.

'Oh God,' said Lee to himself in horror. 'Was that where I went wrong?'

But he could not bear to think that she might desire them both because she thought they were incomplete without each other. He was jealous only of the shared secrets at which they hinted with every glance but, even so, his jealousy was as bitter and humiliating as that which had tortured Buzz during the nights when Lee and Annabel first made love beyond the thin partition. Buzz knew this and was happy. Lee went on marking his books in angry disquiet for now he found he himself had become the sullen interloper; and, at this point, his brother and his wife might themselves have believed they could exclude him from their plottings. But the plot was woven solely to exclude him and so he remained negative but essential.

The sunlight occupied less and less of the room as evening drew on. Lee finished his marking, put on his shirt and prepared to go out for Buzz's lean face grew more and more viciously malign and the heavy air breathed antagonism. But Buzz and Annabel got to their feet, also, as if mutually consenting to carry on the torment a little longer, and they drifted downstairs together, out into the golden evening. In the street, Buzz took care to walk between Lee and the girl to emphasize how emphatically he divided them. But still they would not let Lee go.

'I need a drink,' said Lee sharply.

Fortunately, there was a group of old acquaintances gathered already in the saloon bar so all three could take their places among them as in the old days and pretend for a while that nothing was happening. The girl, Carolyn, sat with her new lover and saw the Collins brothers and their wife come in. She had not seen Lee since the night Buzz broke her nose. She had hoped she would never see any of them again, trailing behind them their slimy snail trails of squalid passion. Lee recognized her and saw how ostentatiously she refused to look at him; he was glad of that for he was in no mood to cope with further complexities.

The bar was crowded with men and women, many of whom he knew and had often talked with in the past. He sat at a table around which were seated people who might think of themselves as friends of his but who seemed devoted solely to the pursuit of contactless sociability, as if this was the best that could be hoped for from human intercourse, gossiping away as if their lives depended on it and, a few feet away, sat a woman who had loved him once and was still so disturbed to find herself unexpectedly in his presence that she refused to acknowledge him. His wife stared into the middle distance in a state, apparently, of luminous vacancy; her lips drooped open a little in half a smile and Lee remembered coming home and finding her in tears because he was not beside her. In the earliest days of their

85

association, her presence had seemed the key to all enigmas; now she was an enigma herself. She was the only one amongst the whole crowd to whom Lee wished to speak but he could find not one word to say to her.

In the course of a spirited conversation which expressed nothing but a common need to pass the time, Buzz reached out his hand and grasped a lock of Annabel's hair. Everybody noticed but everybody went on talking with redoubled vigour. As, entirely without surprise, she turned to Buzz, he drew her towards him by his handful of her hair and kissed her for a long, long time. Then he pushed back his chair and rose; she took his hand and they went out together. As soon as they were outside the bar, they embraced again. Their single, merged silhouette flashed up against the glass door and vanished.

They left a vivid hush behind them. The disruption of decorum took place so abruptly nobody was in the least prepared for it or knew how the gaping hole in the fabric of everyday behaviour could possibly be repaired. Some kinds of collective embarrassment reach such an orgasmic peak the participants cannot recover easily from the crisis and relapse into prolonged discomfort. Those around the table fumbled with their beer mats and avoided the sight of the presumably outraged husband who lost face so entirely he no longer looked in the least as anybody remembered him, for his mouth was twisted in a vile, cynical grin and his reddened eyes were angry as raw wounds. He pulled himself to his feet, knocking over a chair.

'Don't –' said a woman, clutching at his sleeve; the Collinses were famous for their violent passions. He remembered how useful his dazzling smile had been in emergencies and, after an immense effort, produced it again.

'It's all right, ducks, I haven't the slightest desire to do him over,' he said with as much poise as he could. The atmosphere began to ease. The brothers' reputation for picturesque and shameless behaviour made the event more acceptable, a public confession of private deviances their friends had always suspected.

Lee wove his way through the crowded tables, nodding and smiling to acquaintances as he went; he managed to put on a fairly adequate show of insouciance but once he found himself in the open air he collapsed against the wall and slid to the ground. After a while, the gentle pressure of a hand on his shoulder announced the presence of the girl, Carolyn. He was not surprised to see her but guessed she intended to comfort him. This made him suspicious of her. She sat down on the ground beside him and did not say anything for a while. It was a beautiful evening; the sky was deep green with a lonely star or two. He looked at Carolyn sideways and was pleased to see her nose had mended perfectly without leaving any kind of scar.

'It was terrible of them to do that to you,' she said. She construed the event in the bar according to the motives she ascribed to Annabel whom she still saw as impelled by a need to punish and shame Lee because of Lee's affair with herself, a perfectly natural interpretation even if quite wrong. She hardly bothered to concern herself with Buzz's motives for she did not know him well and concluded only that he was sick, which excused everything and made it unnecessary to look further for causes of his aberrations. Lee had no desire to discuss his brother's abduction of his wife. He tried to change the subject. He cleared his throat.

'I saw you with that bloke, I thought you weren't speaking to me.'

'I was afraid you might do something stupid so I came out, just to see you, to see you were all right.'

'Something stupid such as what?'

'I don't know,' she said, faltering a little for he seemed so calm and reasonable violence was out of the question, and she might have followed him only from a need to reinstate herself with him. Because this might, in fact, be so, she grew a little uneasy but Lee wanted to illuminate the situation for her in depth. He was deceived by her concern and thought it was for Annabel, since Annabel was his principal concern, and we always think that others must have the same compulsive interest in our private perturbations as we do ourselves.

'She's probably bitten off more than she can handle, see. I've known him longer than she has, I know all sorts of things about him she's never bothered herself with and probably wouldn't understand, anyway, like how he feels about our mum, for instance. Our mum, see, she thought he was the Anti-Christ, he was only so high and she thought he leaked out poisons.'

He noticed his schoolteacher accent had vanished completely and found himself talking to Carolyn with the frantic desperation of the lonely; he gave her a last, explanatory sentence and stopped short, from pride.

'But I can't stop her trying it with Buzz, if she wants.'

'Then why are you crying?' For his eyes were watering, partly due to the smoke in the bar.

'Of course I'm crying,' he snapped. She misunderstood him completely for she did not know about his eye infection and took his tears at face value. She spoke in a muffled, distantly disappointed voice for it is always hard to acknowledge one has been a second-string lover, even when the affair is over.

'You really do love her, don't you?'

Whether he did or not seemed entirely beside the point to Lee and he snarled at her: 'Shall we discuss it?' Carolyn picked at a thread in her skirt, chilled at his unexpected irritation, and Lee remorsefully put his arm round her and drew her against his shoulders. She rested her cheek thankfully against his throat but did not look up at him and, after a while, spoke his name rather sadly.

'Lee . . .'

'Yeah?'

'I had an abortion.'

'Well,' said Lee, at a loss. 'Well, well.'

There was a pause. During this pause, a very pure moon sailed into the sky. It was now as difficult as it was necessary to carry on the conversation.

'Why didn't you tell me?'

'What could you have done?'

'I dunno. Given you money or something. Been supportive in some way.'

He tried to normalize the revelation by giving her a brilliant smile but still she kept her eyes fixed on her fingertips and did not see it.

'Is that all you can say?' she said in a low, almost a choking voice. It seemed to her Lee had forcibly subjected her to monstrous excesses of fear, pain and feeling which, now all was over between them, were like memories of a trip to another planet and she needed a little reassurance that the excursion had not been a waste of time, for surely what had happened to her had been significant; only, she did not know in the least what it could have meant.

'What do you want me to say?' asked Lee gently for he was prepared to say anything that would comfort her if it meant she would go away more quickly and leave him by himself.

'Oh, please,' she said. 'I did love you, really, I did.'

Whether she said this because it was true or because the confession or reminder of the connection which, however briefly, had existed between them might be a clue to the meaning she sought, she did not know; nevertheless, it was a kind of coercion which Lee's sentimentality could not withstand. He began to feel sadly protective towards her.

'When did you find out you were pregnant?'

'Just before Easter. It couldn't have been anyone but you,' she added wistfully. Lee's sadness turned into misery.

'She was still in the madhouse, then. Was that why you didn't tell me?'

'Yes,' she said with a sudden plucky little jerk of the head that implied hitherto unexplored dimensions of feminine grit. Lee experienced an instant revulsion.

'That was terribly, terribly brave and thoughtful of you,' he said so sardonically she was shocked. He decided to undervalue her self-sacrifice as much as he was able.

'I'll tell you what I'd have done if you'd told me. I'd have left

89

Annabel for good and gone to live with you, if you wanted me to, that is, and looked after you and the kid and so on to the best of my ability. Yeah, that's what I'd have done.'

She did not believe him at all.

'Come now,' she said with a certain irony for she knew she herself had acted for the best. 'What would you *really* have done?'

'Oh, it's all hypothetical. That was then and this is now and how can I tell what I would have done, really? I might have moved in with you, that might have been my duty. On the other hand, I might have jumped into the river to escape my conflicting obligations.'

'You've become terribly bitter,' she said.

'At least mad people don't talk such banalities,' he complained fretfully, annoyed by the implication she herself had remained unembittered by misfortune.

'You never cared for me at all, not seriously,' she said. Lee was quite befogged by a dialogue taking place in a language he did not fully understand for it was that of defensive emotional exploration. He shook his head to clear it and tried to answer her with a satisfactory degree of truth.

'It was like as if you offered me a one-way ticket to normalcy. So of course I cared for you. And I would have lived with you, if you would have had me.'

At that moment, it seemed to him very likely he would indeed have done so, had it not been quite impossible. His voice was so steady and serious she was completely convinced by him and felt an immense nostalgia for her unnecessary misery; besides, he was still beautiful enough and, at the moment, sufficiently pitiable to move her. On the other hand, he was no longer a constant presence in her life but only a visitor from a time that was now gone for good; he was a revenant who no longer affected her. She reverted to the theme of his public humiliation for it was all there was left to talk about.

'It was terrible of them to do that to you.'

Lee shifted his attention back to his brother and his wife.

'It's ironic, yes.'

'I've got someone else to love, you know,' she said almost apologetically and that, too, was ironic.

'Go back to your new bloke, then. He'll be wondering what's become of you.'

But she could not leave him alone.

'Where shall you go?'

'Back home and wait for her.'

Carolyn was astonished.

'Wait for her?'

'Oh, she'll be back,' said Lee with a certain melancholy. 'She'll be back in a state of anguish in about two hours' time, I reckon, though possibly a little before.'

'Oh, darling, do come back with us,' she said with well-bred solicitude for she could patronize him now he was helpless. 'I don't like to think of you, deserted, in that dreadful flat.'

Either because she had kept an excuse to leave Annabel for good to herself or, perhaps, because he would not stand for criticism of his wife in any circumstances, even if she was out of her wits, Lee now felt richly murderous towards Carolyn. He put on a display of ill-tempered bad taste, pulled himself together and went home.

'Shall I come back for coffee then? Can we watch television or shall I chat with your bloke about abortion-law reform?'

*

Buzz and Annabel shared a twined silence until the key turned in the door of the familiar but unknown room, and, for a moment, they interrupted their embrace in a mutual hesitation when they found they had arrived so quickly at the locale of its conclusion. Their surroundings were just as Annabel had imagined them; she checked with a mental inventory the peeling walls, bare and lopsided staircase, fissured linoleum underfoot, foetid accumulated reek of years of the greasy cookery of the poor and the single bulb which meanly leaked a dim light. She found she had overlooked no desolate detail. She shuddered with anticipation not so much to know she was near to assuaging a longing but that consummation would be accomplished in the place she herself had created for it.

The windows of his room were pasted over with sheets of black paper and the meagre sticks of landladies' furniture were hidden by the detritus of his obsessions. The stained, brownish wallpaper was pinned everywhere with photographs of Lee and herself, of herself alone and of Lee alone. Lee had once possessed the rare knack of looking exactly like himself when photographed; his self-consciousness made it inevitable. She had not expected to see so many photographs of Lee. They represented, now, a fissure of tiny cracks in her scrupulous imaginary edifice. Nevertheless, she braved out his hundred eyes and stretched at once on the narrow, unmade bed where, as she expected, the sheets were yellow with use. Then began the slow decline of her hopes.

At first, she could not help smiling the easy smile which, if all went well on her own terms, might become her natural expression but Buzz did not speak and did not lie down beside her and, eager as she was to touch him, she grew uneasy. She knew no way to break the sudden constraint between them except by speaking herself and she did not know what to say nor what he might reply. Buzz kept as far away from the bed as the constricted space would allow and his heavy lids drooped down over his eyes with foreboding for, now he had indulged his spite against his brother, he was left to face the consequences of it alone.

If jealousy or, rather, resentment of Lee had primarily moved him, his revenge would still be incomplete unless he recreated the maddening acts his inward eye had witnessed so atrociously as he lay beyond the thin wall, sweating at the sound of their voices. He always saw her only in relation to his brother; his interest in her was based on the knowledge he could utilize her both to defend himself against Lee and also to attack him through her after, first of all, she had usurped Buzz in his own home and his brother's affections and then turned him out of both. Now it came to the testing, he would have sworn their shared games and mutual secrets were only so many exercises in manoeuvres although, at the time, he had cultivated them for their own sake, to pass the time; and if, incidentally, he estranged her from her husband and his brother from himself, that served to pass the time, also, in a way that suited his taste for dark corners and circuitous routes. But he only decided to hate his brother when Lee refused to live with him any more, and now, after a few months' passionate imaginings, he believed himself moved only by hatred. He had forgotten or never realized that Annabel had credited him with the attributes of a saviour and had she told him so as she lay on his bed things might have turned out better; or else, far worse.

As it was, he faltered between her real self on the bed and her many shadows on the wall, determined to have her but thwarted by his inability to feel as intensely in situations that were actual as he did in the supercharged events of his imagination. Life rarely rose to the demands he made on it. He tried to stimulate himself with memories of past sexual dreams and encounters and found himself as if rummaging in a forbidden cupboard of grotesqueries until he found a memory of Annabel prone on a tiled floor with her blood welling out through the silk pores of her embroidered shawl while, as he still believed, Lee lay in some other woman's bed. This idea alone filled him with desire.

He had often seen her naked but he had never handled her cold breasts nor touched sufficient of her skin to discover how closely its texture, that of chilled rice paper, corresponded to its colour. Nor had he known she would fling out her arms in an attitude of subjugation or death and lie so unnaturally still. The more he caressed her, the stiffer and colder she seemed to grow as if her huge, grey eyes divined in his the true reflection of the perverse origins of his desire and so she made her body act out the role he had devised although she believed that all she wanted for herself would be to surrender to simple, voluptuous actuality. She wanted this desperately. So they began a duel of mismatched expectancies in which Annabel was bound to be the worst hurt for her hopes had been literally infinite while his, true to his nature, existed only in the two dimensions and glaring colours of melodrama.

But he had not bargained for his own horror which increased with every moment of her passivity and the excitement which contained within it such a high degree of dread. He turned over her limp hand and, seeing the faint, white scars on her wrist, found he could manage to kiss her only to discover her lips were made of ice and her tongue burned like freezing metal. His mother who assured her small, dark son with the infernal conviction of the insane that he was the fruit of all the evil in the world had given him many fears about the physicality of women; all the nightmares that had ever visited him rushed back into his head at once and he flinched back from Annabel's mouth, which numbed him.

'Open your legs,' he said. 'Let me look.'

She did as he asked her, faintly wondering, as she had once been with Lee, and already confronted with a great divergence between her desires and her actuality. Buzz crouched between her feet and scrutinized as much as he could see of her perilous interior to find out if all was in order and there were no concealed fangs or guillotines inside her to ruin him. Although he found no visual evidence, he remained too suspicious of her body to wish to meet her eyes so he caught hold of her shoulders and roughly pushed her down on her face. She was astonished; she felt herself handled as unceremoniously as a fish on a slab, reduced only to anonymous flesh, and she could do nothing to help herself for she knew she had connived in her own undoing. He thrust at her from behind and it was all over in a few seconds; he came as soon as he clumsily pushed his way into her and instantly withdrew, in a convulsive movement like a gigantic wince.

She cowered in his rancid bed. He mumbled something she did not understand and pulled the sheet up over her, to hide her, but when his hand accidentally touched her hair, he jumped back. They had imagined too often and too much and so they had exhausted all their possibilities. When they embraced each other's phantoms, each in his separate privacy had savoured the most refined of pleasures but, connoisseurs of unreality as they were, they could not bear the crude weight, the rank smell and the ripe taste of real flesh. It is always a dangerous experiment to act out a fantasy; they had undertaken the experiment rashly and had failed but Annabel suffered the worst for she had been trying to convince herself she was alive.

She cowered in his rancid bed and whispered: 'I want to go home,' for the only solace she could envisage was to pretend this bitterest of disappointments was itself a dream and that, when it grew light, Buzz's dark, strange body would revert to the familiar shape of her husband for she had often pretended the one was the other, anyway. Buzz covered his face with his hands and allowed her to dress herself and wander off alone through the dark streets, a fragile, flimsy thing whose body had betrayed both their imaginations.

As she came into the kitchen, Lee was burning his three precious photographs by holding a match to the tip of each; he watched while the blue flame blackened the picture and then he dropped each withered scrap into the sink and turned the tap so that the ashes were washed down the drain. She took a cup from the dresser, went past him to fill it with water, and drank. Torn between jealousy and suppressed murderous rage, Lee was in an evil mood and quite prepared to eschew compassion; he saw only that she was in a state where it might be possible to injure her and at once struck out.

'But what did he do to you? What did he actually do? Did he ask you to lift up his tail and kiss his asshole?'

She shook her head dumbly and Lee doubled up with unpleasant laughter.

'When he was living with my aunt, it was the summer she died, he brought this young chick back and took her up to his room and I was getting the old lady her Benger's food in the kitchen and there was this crash, this terrible crash, like someone falling downstairs, and the kitchen door burst open, didn't it. And this chick fell right through it, she was stark naked and she was clutching her knickers in her hand and she said: "If he thinks I'm going to do that, he's very much mistaken."'

'I would have done anything for him, if he had let me,' said Annabel gravely. Lee saw she did not understand he was jeering at her and opened his mouth to make a more direct and brutal attack; then he shrugged and said nothing for clearly she would pay him no attention. He grew less vindictive when he saw how dazed and spiritless she was and would have tried to comfort her if he had known how and had he ever before been able to succeed in comforting her.

She rinsed out her cup and put it upside down on the draining board. She went into the bedroom, walking extremely carefully, for she was about to play her last hand and must concentrate very hard on repressing her panic; she had decided to seduce him.

Avoiding his eyes, she took off her clothes, hurried and quickly hid herself on the far side of the bed so that he would suspect nothing. He thought she was unconsciously instructing him that now her body was out of bounds and, as he undressed more slowly, he said to himself: 'It's probably all over between her and me, she'll probably never let me screw her again.' And this was a great relief for the notion he might by chance encounter even so much as a stray limb of hers under the covers that night filled him with disgust. He stretched out bitterly in the dark beside her, resigned to emptiness, only to discover she had been cunningly lying in wait for him all the time.

She flung herself upon him in a startling rush. She glued herself to his mouth, breast and belly, moaning and sobbing. He thrashed this way and that to shake her off but she clung too desperately to be shifted and the dark splintered in Lee's head as, apparently beside herself, she twisted against him in a sinister frenzy, speaking his name relentlessly in a hot, dry voice he had never heard from her before. In the folklore of Haiti, there exist female demons named *diablesses* who are so avid for pleasure they seduce the living only to abandon them at the end of the lascivious night among the white graves of a cemetery. So, in the dark, a changeling Annabel attacked Lee with gross, morbid passion and such a barrage of teeth and nails he struck her on the side of the head to stop her inflicting any more damage. She howled with surprise and affront and, continuing to howl, tumbled down on him in a stinging shower of disordered hair.

'I wish you were dead,' said Lee. She stopped howling and murmured indistinguishable sounds as she lavished kisses on his throat and shoulders, until soon he caught her fever, turned her on to her back and penetrated her. First, she twitched a little, and muttered; and then she wound her arms around him with bizarre, conciliatory tenderness, pressing her small breasts against the green name she had inscribed upon his bosom and begging him to stop, for now she was afraid he might take her too far, would take her to a place where she might lose herself.

'Please,' she said. 'Don't go on, I don't think I can bear it, not now. Not tonight, I was mistaken when I wanted it.'

'Oh no, my love,' said Lee, intent on the unforgivable. 'This time you'll get what's coming to you, you will.'

Nevertheless, it proved a mutual rape. She expelled her breath in a wavering sigh and seemed to fall limply away from him but, as soon as he began to move inside her, her response was immediate and, it seemed, out of her control. She cried out in a lonely voice and bit and tore at him so savagely he wondered if he would survive the night for he had never known a more tempestuous performance from anyone and, in the dark, she could have been a stranger. He had never been superstitious in his life before but, after it was over, he turned on the light to look at her, for her behaviour had no place in the order of things.

It was his Annabel, still, although she was as bruised and bleeding as himself. She was his Annabel, compounded of memory, so he stroked her hair remorsefully and pressed his burning eyes against her cool skin; yet he had truly wished her dead, for then he would no longer have to care about her.

'I'm afraid I've invested all my emotional capital in you,' he said. 'And that's all I can say, though God help the small investor

97

when the revolution comes. Though I wouldn't say I was a small investor. So I suppose it would be even worse.'

She did not hear one word and when his eyes met hers, he was struck by their curious expression, one of perplexity mingled with assessment. He knew she must be thinking of his brother and guessed she had been deceiving him all the time although he did not know why.

In his late adolescence, at a party, on a pile of coats on somebody else's bed, he held a girl in his arms and kissed her while Buzz copulated with her, glancing up at him from time to time as if for approval. When Buzz wandered off afterwards he and the girl made love with the enthusiasm of transgressors. He had forgotten her face and never knew her name; he remembered only that something like that had taken place and the circumstances and the residual traces of his brother on the nameless girl's body had given him a peculiar satisfaction. It was an adventure similar to many others at that time when nothing he had done was unnatural, and it had never entered his head for years, not until now, when it seemed he would never again sleep with his wife without his brother's invisible company.

'Once,' said Annabel, 'I came home and found you and Buzz together on the floor, curled up in each other's arms like happy puppies.'

'We've always been like cowboys and Indians to each other, we must have been fighting.' But Lee was discomfited to find she could reflect and enlarge upon his thoughts. She paid no attention to him. She invented her own connections between the past and the present.

'He didn't even take his clothes off,' said Annabel who had no sense of the ridiculous.

'He's got few, if any, refinements. Don't blame me for his incapacities. He's always been funny with girls, I told you.'

'Then how did he get gonorrhoea in North Africa, that time?'

'I hate to think,' said Lee. 'Though there aren't too many ways of getting the clap that I know of. But he couldn't even put his finger inside a sea anemone at one time, for fear of engulfment.'

'Whyever should he want to put his finger in a sea anemone?' she marvelled and lay beside him in a miserable silence for a long while, till he thought she might be sleeping and reached out to turn off the light. At that, she threw her arm over him and pinned him down again.

'Lee . . . tell me . . .'

'What is it now?' he asked uneasily.

'Is that what it's supposed to be like?'

'No,' said Lee in order to hurt her if he could. 'That's what it's usually like, with normal women.'

Her smile faded, her eyes dilated with woe and she drew back.

'Then Buzz could have made it properly with me if you had been there,' she said with exquisite dismay and took her pale web of flesh away from him to the farthest edge of the bed. His eyes became so painful he could not see her any more but could make out only an indistinct mass of brown hair which could have been shaved from an unknown head and dumped on the pillow. The hair began to shudder like a nest of incipient snakes.

'It's no good!' exclaimed Lee and fell from the bed. Though the distance to the floor was no more than two or three feet, he seemed to fall into a bottomless pit and was surprised to hit the floorboards so soon. He dragged down the bedside lamp with him by the flex and left everything behind him plunged in darkness.

*

Stirred by the odorous breezes of the night, the undergrowth in the park rustled a little as if each bush contained a pair of somnolent lovers and the air smelled sweetly of crushed grass. The summer moon distilled almost too honeyed a light for moonlight and Lee, who would have preferred a storm with thunderbolts, stumbled angrily into this sweet quiescence and, on the crest of a hill, lost all impetus for renewed flight although, when he was a child, he got as far as Southampton in the pursuit of liberty. He collapsed on a bench in the white shadow of the

Gothic tower and buried his head in his hands. He felt nothing but the absence of feeling which is despair.

After a while, he heard a faint, shifting patter of footsteps on gravel and then, behind him, the sound of moist, noisy, loud and intimate breathing like the shameless breathing of a bad-mannered child. The breathing was interspersed with small giggles. Lee ignored whatever hovered behind him until, smitten with the urge to perform an infant's trick, it clapped its hands over Lee's eyes. Lee grasped the bony wrist and wrenched it until the sinews cracked. The intruder yelped and Lee, turning to look at him, saw a young boy with wild eyes and floating hair, clearly another mad person who might have been the crazed inhabitant of the Gothic pinnacle which, appropriately enough, served as the backdrop for their balked encounter. Lee let the boy go and he tenderly rubbed his bruises, casting reproachful glances at Lee from time to time although his giggling changed to a soft, wordless whine as he edged coyly round the bench and gingerly sat himself down. The sight of his thin face reminded Lee how, when he collected Annabel, a boy on the hospital porch questioned him about the tarot pack.

'I see you fled the Fool's Tower, then,' said Lee who guessed the boy was adding to his troubles by the use of some sort of hallucinogen. The boy nodded vigorously and tried to reply but an incoherent babble of sounds came out of his mouth and he made no sense at all. A sharp spasm of distress shook him from head to toe and he shielded his working face with an arm in a ripped shirtsleeve.

'Do you want a cigarette?'

The boy blindly stretched out his hand. Lee gave him the remainder of the packet and also a box of matches. The boy pocketed them without looking at them.

'Do you need any money?'

The boy nodded. Lee found he had two pound notes and about fifteen shillings in change. The boy accepted the money without thanks or enthusiasm. Lee wondered what he could give him and remembered his wedding ring. This time, the boy displayed a brief flicker of curiosity when he saw the gold band on his palm. Lee spoke in a leaden, didactic, schoolteacher's voice.

'Me and my wife have fallen into the habit of performing symbolic actions with our wedding rings. She ate hers.'

The boy raised his shaggy head and stared at him. By the light of the moon, he must have seen the huge, scarlet-pricked, purplish, diabolical bite on Lee's neck for he raised his eyebrows, leaned forward and touched it delicately and enquiringly with his fingertips. He giggled again, this time with a faint note of interrogation. He smelled horribly of mud and excrement.

'She carried on the metaphor by trying to eat me alive,' said Lee. 'I got away just in time.'

Dear God, he thought, I'm starting to dramatize myself. The boy shrugged. He made several thwarted attempts to speak but could produce no sensible sounds of any kind and at last wept unrestrainedly until his scratched, scabbed face was blubbered with tears and snot. Lee thought he must somehow have hired the boy to act out his ugly grief for him, like a professional mourner, now he himself had grown so cold and mechanical, lulled by the strange narcotic of a steady, quiet anguish. He had nothing with which to dry the boy's eyes, either, and so he must wait until the mysterious spring of tears dried up. The boy bobbed about on the bench in an uncoordinated fashion until he let out a wind-bell tinkle of pitiful since joyless laughter, sprang up and darted off the way he had come.

In the sequence of events which now drew the two brothers and the girl down, in ever-decreasing spirals, to the empty place at the centre of the labyrinth they had built between them, this nameless boy performed the function of the fool in the Elizabethan drama, a reference point outside events but inside another kind of logic, the remorseless logic of unreason where all vision is deranged, all action uncoordinated and all responses beyond prediction. Such logic now dominated Annabel.

She searched through her rooms with the sightless hands of a somnambulist until she found the tablets Lee gave to Buzz to make him sleep and discovered only four remained in the bottle. Though they would grant her only limited relief, she swallowed them and chose to lie down on the sofa rather than return to the bed where she had so recently been confounded. In spite of the barbiturates, she slept lightly and fitfully, visited by dreams she always took for memories so that, when she woke in the morning, she recalled how she had been married in church and the dress of black crêpe her parents bought her, an ensemble completed by a thick veil of the kind worn by widowed queens. They pressed a bunch of dead roses into her hands while the organ played 'Eternal Father, Strong to Save' and Lee grew in size until his golden body filled the vaulted building and was soon transformed into the building itself.

The morning was as beautiful as the night which preceded it and she prepared a small breakfast in the sunny kitchen. She set out two places and decided that, if Lee came home by eight o'clock, she would not kill herself. At five past eight, she heard his footstep on the stairs but she had already hung his cup back on the dresser and put plate and saucer on the shelf.

When Lee saw her unexpected serenity, he wondered if she had forgotten the night entirely or had subjected it to the force of her imagination and turned it to her own benefit so she could go on. All might continue as it had done before or shift so imperceptibly from bad to worse he might barely notice it. He asked her for money for his day's expenses and she could find none in her bag so she sent him to her money box. It was stuffed so full of notes the lid scarcely fitted any more and after Lee went off to work she shook out all the money on the bedroom floor and sat cross-legged to count it all out by the light that came through the cracks in the boards across the window. There was more than forty pounds in the tin.

Because her wedding dress was black, she chose a long, plain, white dress of cotton with a square-cut neck and long, tight sleeves. In the mirror of the changing room in the shop, she glimpsed the possibility of another perfect stranger, one as indifferent to the obscene flowers of the flesh as drowned

Ophelia, so she had her hair dyed to dissociate her new body from the old one even more and then she got her face painted in a beauty shop. She was surprised to see how cold, hard and impersonal this new face was. What notes remained from her shopping spree she tore up into little pieces. It was now the mellow time of late afternoon.

She took out her old sketchbooks and fingered wistfully through them for every stroke of crayon or pencil had once been alive to her; her pictures had never referred to the objects they might have seemed to represent but, to her, had been palpable things themselves. But she could not draw anything any more and so was forced to make these imaginative experiments with her own body which were now about to culminate, finally, in erasure, for she had failed in the attempt to make herself the living portrait of a girl who had never existed. From time to time she started when she heard voices in the flat above or the noises of the street outside seeped thinly through the opaque windows. She was troubled by an over-acuteness of the senses and wondered why they shouted so loudly upstairs or the cars outside made, today, such tigerish roarings. She was irritated rather than disturbed to sense occasionally the almost inarticulate breathings and the infinitely subtle movements of the figures on the walls and her sudden excess of sensibility made the paper between her fingers coarser than sandpaper. She saw pits and bristles where the pores and hairs were on the skin of her forearm. Before she had finished looking through her books, Lee came home again.

'What are you doing here?' she demanded angrily.

He would have said the same himself if she had given him time to speak for at first glance he did not recognize her. By some extraordinary chance, she had chosen to colour her hair the same shade of polished brass the woman doctor in the hospital used but her black-rimmed eyes, sweeping lashes, arched brows, carmined lips and dark red fingernails were those of the earliest memories of his mother, before she took up a more flamboyant style of make-up; she wore a white dress cut like the nightdress in which his aunt had been buried; but she sat among a pile of drawings in a manner which recalled only Annabel and so he finally identified this composite figure with his wife, though he was so dazed with sleeplessness he could have been hallucinating her. While he was out in the plain air of school, it seemed hardly possible she could wholly have transformed herself so that nothing remained familiar about her except for certain spiky gestures of her hands.

He was so struck by the newly adamantine brilliance of her eyes he did not see they no longer reflected anything. With her glittering hair and unfathomable face, streaked with synthetic red, white and black, she looked like nothing so much as one of those strange and splendid figures with which the connoisseurs of the baroque period loved to decorate their artificial caves, those *atlantes composés* fabricated from rare marbles and semi-precious stones. She had become a marvellous crystallization retaining nothing of the remembered woman but her form, for all the elements of which this new structure were composed had suffered a change, the eyes put out by zircons or spinels, the hair respun from threads of gold and the mouth enamelled scarlet. No longer vulnerable flesh and blood, she was altered to inflexible material. She could have stepped up into the jungle on the walls and not looked out of place beside the tree with breasts or the carnivorous flowers for now she was her own, omnipotent white queen and could move to any position on the board.

'Go away,' she said to Lee. 'Leave me alone.'

'Dear God,' said Lee. '*Le jour de gloire est arrivé.*'

Inevitably, he began to laugh at such a reversal for the revolution which he both feared and longed for had arrived at last and he was reduced to bankruptcy for there was nothing left for him to love in this magnificent creature. All would not, now, continue in the old style for she dismissed him without a blessing.

'Go away,' she repeated. 'Don't come back, don't ever come back. I don't want any more to do with you.'

She was extraordinarily beautiful and radiated a gripping air of excitement; Lee soon ceased to laugh for he was seized with the conviction she had dressed herself up so splendidly only for the sake of his brother.

'Has he been back, then? Did you come to terms, you and him?'

'Why are you waiting?' she said. 'Get out.'

He was furious to find how much he was weeping, as if his eyes were dazzled and he choked on a farewell, shrugged, dropped his briefcase on the floor and left her to herself, though he had only nine shillings and sixpence in the world and nowhere else to go.

She was hardly aware who he was, unless he were a materialization of a picture from her books; she had even forgotten she had branded him. When she bent down over the page again, a lock of yellow hair fell forward with a soft plop onto a sketch of the chief of the Mohawks walking on a roof and she bit back a scream for she saw a yellow snake and heard a thud. Only when she touched the snake with her finger did she realize it was only her own hair though this, too, seemed an unnatural substance now it was so yellow. Then she became aware of a slow, rhythmic banging which must be her own heartbeat and soon she heard the brisk drumming of her pulse. She waited impatiently for it to grow dark because her excited senses turned the vigil into an ordeal; when it grew dark, she would go into the bedroom, seal the double doors with adhesive tape, turn on the rusted gas outlets above the mantelpiece, lie down on the bed and suffer herself to be blotted out but she thought, this night of all nights, perhaps the sun might never stop shining. At that, she moaned with terror and panic. There were no clocks in the flat so she could not tell whether or not time was passing.

Now he had been granted his liberty, Lee did not know what to do with it. He sat on the kerb outside his former home for a while, shielding his eyes from the sun, anaesthetized by sleeplessness and shock. Because he could think of nowhere else to go, he went to the park and slept on the grass for three or four hours. He woke up in the cool, blue dusk which signed Annabel's order of release. He was hungry and went down towards the dock road, looking for a café, as she scraped a flake of varnish from her fingernail while she taped the tops of the doors and tsk'd with annoyance for she wanted to look perfect on her deathbed. But then she thought perhaps a minor imperfection would make the spectacle even more touching and, besides, the important thing was to get it all over with and not mind too much about impressions for the quality of death would make her impressive enough in itself. She put clean sheets on the bed for last night's were printed all over with false passions and she did not want to die in the bedclothes between which she had used her body and her imagination to extricate herself from her fantasies and failed at it so badly. The arrival of night, on schedule, had given her some confidence and she worked quickly and eagerly. In the café, Lee fell into conversation with two bored lorry drivers playing a fruit machine and, before long, found himself in a bar.

It was a glum and barren place though an old man played upon an out-of-tune piano and a group of exhausted whores now and then broke into song. Lee drank the drinks the lorry drivers bought him and let a whore reveal her teeth to him in thin, smiling chatter that fell on his ears like the pattering of raindrops. Unfamiliar as he was with the phenomenon of rejection, he could only diagnose his condition as one of positive grief modified by indignation and he cast around for some retributive act or, at least, an invitation from a stranger to cancel out his dismissal and restore his self-esteem.

As if on cue, as his indignation reached its peak, into the bar came the girl Joanne, always an unexpected apparition, sulky as ever and more voluptuous than he remembered unless he garnished her with a little extra voluptuousness because his antennae indicated she was available. She was immediately aware of Lee, though she said a few words, perhaps imparting a message, to a middle-aged man seated in a corner with a sodden group before she came over to her teacher and took up such an aggressively defensive stance before him he had no idea she shook with nerves to find him accessible and alone. Her semi-circular eyebrows gave her bland, white, motionless face the look of a screen star of the thirties. The piano player thumped out 'Roses of Picardy' and Lee knew everything was stale, boring and inevitable; he would seduce this trusting child to once more validate his amorality and again find himself in a swamp of self-disgust so he gave her his dazzling smile and waited for her to sit down beside him, in order that the action should commence.

She wore a tight, short dress of a vulgar, printed material and Lee, indulging a dislike of her which considerably sharpened his intentions, thought how he had short-circuited the time scale of the old saw, 'From clogs to clogs in three generations'. She was one of the back-street bad girls of his teens and, now Annabel had deserted him, he would revert irretrievably to type, throw up his job and education, join, perhaps, the Merchant Navy or go to work on a building site. He was ravenous for the commonplace. Saturday's fight gave her the chance to accost him at last; she thanked him in a breathy, almost diffident manner, shifting from foot to foot, before seating herself on the torn, plastic-covered bench, taking great care she did not touch him.

'That's my dad,' she said suddenly, indicating the drunken middle-aged man with a jerk of her head. 'He's in here every night, the old soak.'

There was no affection in her voice.

'Where does your mother go?'

'She's dead,' she said without emotion. They were the family of whom the street was a little ashamed, the boozing father who made complicated deals about second-hand cars and his farouche, sluttish daughter, who lived discontentedly together and often brawled in a mean house where there was nothing that could be remembered with affection. Avid for the crass, Lee put his hand on her thigh with such a coarse and blatant gesture she started. She had not expected an advance quite so soon for he had rescued her from a similar embarrassment a night or so ago and, besides, he was a schoolteacher although tonight he looked drunk or somehow subtly unlike the presentation of himself he gave in the classroom. Nevertheless, she expected something like finesse, at least, and she snapped: 'Hands off!'

Lee was delighted to hear the fishwife clang in her voice and offered her a drink. She accepted half a pint of shandy and, giggling occasionally, she sipped it, eyeing him over the rim of the glass in a manner which brought back his early youth so strongly he was both attracted and filled with distaste. She was angry with herself because she knew she seemed gauche but she could not help it for she was very unsure of herself. When he gave her a cigarette, she coughed at the first draw and, knowing she had given more evidence of unsophistication, she became withdrawn and sulky. She huddled morosely inside her skimpy dress and looked at him with barely concealed antagonism. But, when her father left the pub, she relaxed visibly; she could behave more freely.

'He's gone off after a deal,' she said and stubbed out the cigarette. As she did so, her susurrating mass of hair brushed his cheek and, spontaneously, without any reference to a putative seduction but only because its friable texture was quite unlike most girls' hair, Lee bit at it to see what such strange, white, flossy hair tasted like. She shivered and tensed, stirred by this unusual advance; then she shrugged, sighed, glanced round to see she was unobserved and kissed him full on the mouth with profligate abandon. Then she sank back away from him on to the bench but she no longer giggled. She stretched out her hands and examined her fingernails, waiting the next move.

Her eyes were pale, ingenuous blue and her fat, soft mouth the colour and somehow the shape of old-fashioned cabbage roses. In conversation, her voice had a harsh, subtly discordant timbre that at times grated unmercifully like the sound of a knife scratched on a plate and her laughter always seemed contemptuous because it was so rasping but she did not speak often and she laughed even less. Beneath the pads of puppy fat which formed a protective mask for the vulnerable forms of what she might become, the lines of her face were inquisitive and, perhaps, demanding. Now and then Lee surprised upon her face an expression of hungry curiosity which might be half desperate to satisfy itself and was probably the explanation of her kiss. Whoever she was, she only played at being a trusting child or else became a trusting child intermittently, when she had no other signposts as to how to act. As she grew more self-assured with Lee and stopped nervously chewing her swollen under-lip all the time, she revealed signs of a sharp, unripe cleverness. Once she was fully embarked on the adventure he represented, she unfolded a few more of her astringent petals and, though she spoke of her father and his ways with a sardonic regret, she did not seem to be unhappy. But she was plainly hungry for new company and, at closing time, it was she who suggested they walk for a while in the park together, the old euphemism, before Lee had a chance to do so.

She had a bounding, springy walk and carried her head so high her voluminous hair followed behind her rather than hung down her back, buoyantly rippling as if imbued with its own share of her energetic grace. She walked like a woman entirely at ease within her skin. Though the sky in the west was still streaked with green and rose, a fornicator's moon beamed down already and, as they entered the park from the south side, Lee, sentimental, cheerful, not altogether cynical and accustomed to making the best of any given set of circumstances, let the guiltless night take control of him.

No shafts of moonlight dared enter the absolute night of Annabel's darkened bedroom as, in darkness, she balanced on a chair to reach the gas taps which were rusted, stiff and difficult to turn. However, she was quite determined. It was an exquisite pleasure to hear the first, faint hiss that announced the inrush of gas into the room. She knew it would take a long time but, like Ophelia, gladly lay down on the river and waited for it to carry her away as if she was light and will-less as a paper boat. She left no notes or messages. She felt no fear or pain for now she was content. She did not spare a thought or waste any pity on the people who loved her for she had never regarded them as anything more than facets of the self she was now about to obliterate so, in a sense, she took them with her to the grave and it was only natural they should now behave as if they had never known her.

But the park was an arena for moonlight and bright as a day without colours. The silver-plated trees cast barely visible shadows on the grass and each blade and daisy, each bud and blossom, shone with an individual, clear, distinct brilliance. The south side of the park was far more luxuriantly wooded than the north and the girl and her man stepped off the path and walked through the moist undergrowth between the bleached trunks of trees, in and out of the stippled light, until they glimpsed before them the serene white pillars of the miniature temple. All was calm, all was bright. The pale light magically rendered Joanne's gaudy dress as a brief tunic of vague, leopard-like blotches and a few twigs and leaves caught in her hair. She looked very young but also very knowing. He was in a mood to be easily attracted by any young woman but anyone would have thought she promised all manner of possibilities as she moved through the dappled wood. She could have been an illusion, a trick of the moon and the perfumed air of midsummer's night, and, indeed, in this aspect of a flowering siren, she was the artificial creation of his habitually romantic imagination. He knew quite well she was a wayward schoolgirl but there are times and places when and where it is a necessary enrichment to trust appearances; and, besides, the knowledge of the tough flesh under the veneer of moonshine was consoling for, whatever she was in reality, she was, one way and another, real.

Annabel was falling asleep, now, slipping into a deep sleep which was a prelude to a coma which was a prelude to nothing and she felt her exterior fading as her outlines ceased to define her. Lee was free to lie down in the grass beside the temple with an amorous girl on the far side of the Gothic north, and when it was late enough for her father to be sleeping in his bed, she took him home with her. They went down into the city through the amoral gates which neither permitted nor denied access, as though the gates themselves negated a moral problem by declaring it improperly phrased. Joanne listened at her bedroom door for her father's snoring while Lee took off his clothes. Her walls were covered with pictures of pop singers and a sash or two from beauty contests hung over the bed; her orange-box furniture was trimmed with frills of mauve tulle but the dirty underwear she kicked hastily beneath the bed proved she was a slut at heart.

But she was a sensitive slut and, now she had got him where she wanted him, she was overcome with belated reticence. She tentatively approached the bed with the hazy movements of a nude walking under water, shaking out the filmy hair that settled on her shoulders in a prickling mass; she always enjoyed smuggling a boyfriend into the house under her father's nose and there was the added temptation of forbidden fruit about this one – her teacher! a married man! – but all at once she was shy of him, because she had inscribed his name again and again at the back of her exercise book for the sheer pleasure of writing it down, had even tried out 'Joanne Collins' on the flyleaf of her civics textbook, then speedily erased it. And she knew enough to know that not by one word or gesture must she reveal she had such a young, foolish crush on him. So she covered her face with her hands and smiled between her fingers in almost an embarrassed way.

Even though all Lee wanted was a little comfort, he felt his heart begin to melt, an experience to which he was no longer accustomed. He held out his arms to her.

She ran her finger over the tattoo on his breast but she did not mention it; three in the bed was one too many for her and she switched off the light so as not to see how he wore his heart on the outside, nor the name on it. In the palpable darkness, all turned out very simple and satisfactory; they were pleased with one another, even though, in the helplessness of sleep, he clung on to her like a drowning man and she had not guessed he would be so desperate for love. That made her uneasy.

She woke him early; he must be out of the house before her father woke and she should finish some neglected homework.

'Sweet Jesus,' thought Lee. 'I've knocked off one of my fifth form.' He probed his conscience for the first twinge of guilt, as one investigates with the tongue a tooth one suspects to be on the point of aching but, try as he would, he could feel no regret. This puzzled him; he was so used to the bulky apparatus of sin and guilt and had forgotten these concepts had never entered his mind until he met Annabel. He arranged to see Joanne in the evening.

'What about your screwy wife, though?' she said with a certain reserve.

'I shouldn't bother your head about her, ducks,' said Lee carelessly. 'After all, she chucked me out, didn't she.'

He had left Annabel in such apparent strength of mind. He had not deserted her for she had rejected him. And, if one should do right because it is right, why should she have been forced to simulate a life-likeness that did not satisfy her? But now she lay in her ultimate, shocking transformation; now she was a painted doll, bluish at the extremities, nobody's responsibility. Lee returned to the house only to retrieve a little money and a few clothes. He found her in the bedroom. Buzz crouched at the end of the bed, at the feet of the bedizened corpse.

'I think you should stand with your foot on her neck,' said Buzz. 'Then I would take your picture with your arms crossed and, you understand, your foot on her neck. Like, in a victorious pose.'

Flies already clustered round her eyes. Buzz had chopped down the boards over the windows but the smell of gas pervaded everything and she was plainly far beyond recovery. Lee struck out at his brother, who crashed from the bed on to the floor. Then they began to squabble drearily as to which of them was most to blame, for nothing but death is irreparable.

AFTERWORD

Love was written in 1969 and the people in it, not quite the children of Marx and Coca-Cola, more the children of Nescafé and the Welfare State, are the pure, perfect products of those days of social mobility and sexual licence. Originally I'd intended to write a little about the novel and how I feel about it after nearly twenty years, how I feel about what seems to me now its almost sinister feat of male impersonation, its icy treatment of the mad girl and its penetrating aroma of unhappiness. And the ornate formalism of the style, that has something to do with where I first got the idea for *Love*, from Benjamin Constant's early-nineteenth-century novel of sensibility, *Adolphe*; I was seized with the desire to write a kind of modern-day, demotic version of *Adolphe*, although I doubt anybody could spot the resemblance after I'd macerated the whole thing in triple-distilled essence of English provincial life.

Then I thought that perhaps the best way of discussing the novel would really be to write a bit more of it. I've changed a lot since 1969, and so has the world; I'm more benign, the world is far bleaker, and the people in *Love* would now be edging nervously up to the middle age they thought could never happen, they thought the world would end first.

I can't resurrect Annabel, of course; even the women's movement would have been no help to her and alternative psychiatry would have only made things, if possible, worse. The novel ends so emphatically, on such an irrefutable statement, that there is something a little tasteless about taking her husband and brother-in-law and the lovers and doctors out of the text that is Annabel's coffin and resurrecting them. But good taste is not a significant attribute of this novel, anyway.

Bit parts first.

Although *the philosophy lecturer's wife* appears only in a cameo role, I feel I did not fully do her justice in the days when I thought that mothers had only themselves to blame. I did not understand why she was so furious. I do, now.

She became a radical feminist in the early seventies and now lives on a remote farm in Wales with three other women, two beautiful AID children (neither of them hers) and a flock of goats. She knows Lee Collins's second wife, Rosie, and also Joanne Davis, q.v., from Greenham Common, but she thinks of her life as a heterosexual as a bad dream from which she is now awake and, besides, Lee was only one of many unsuccessful solutions to her discontent and she never could remember his name unless she looked it up first.

Her husband obtained custody of their three children; she did not contest him. He gained his soul at the price of promotion and publications. He remains in the same job, even in the same flat, but his children rise up and call him blessed and though they are now almost grown he still runs a 'Single Fathers' workshop at the Community Centre of which the coordinator is Rosie Collins.

Lee, incorrectly, suspects them of conducting a sedate and reticent affair. It is worse than that. They have discussed it and decided not to. But it is worse than *that*, even, for the philosophy lecturer's seventeen-year-old son is sleeping with the Collinses' fifteen-year-old daughter on the very bed under the reproduction of the blue-period Picasso harlequin, now somewhat faded. (There is an admirable consistency to provincial life.) Rosie took her to the family planning clinic, but does not tell Lee, as she believes he is capable of homicide where his daughters are concerned.

The peroxided psychiatrist left the NHS for private practice shortly after the events described in this novel, though not before prescribing Lee, after Annabel's suicide, tranquillizers of such strength in such quantities that he became a virtual zombie.

She is now on the board of directors of a consortium that runs a chain of extremely expensive detoxification centres for very rich junkies. She is also a director of three pharmaceutical companies, hosts a radio phone-in on neurosis and is author of a nonfiction bestseller, *How to Succeed Even Though You Are a Woman*. She is a passionate advocate of hormone-replacement therapy. She drives a Porsche, rather fast.

Joanne Davis had too much brute sense of self-preservation to have anything more to do with Lee after she found out what had happened. While he was absent on compassionate leave, she removed herself from school and ran away from home to London.

A man she met on the train got her a job as a hostess in a near-beer club in Soho. From there she graduated successfully to stripping and made a modest killing as a model in the early days of soft porn magazines in the seventies, putting sufficient by to take out a mortgage on a flat in one of the mansion blocks along the Finchley Road and make the down payment on a sports car. This comfortable life came to an abrupt end when she became pregnant as the result of a cash transaction with a minor Saudi princeling.

After her abortion, she felt that if her life was indeed worth more than that of the child she had been carrying, she could no longer continue to take off her clothes for money but must find some other work. No job that did not involve her sexuality offered enough income to keep up the repayments on her smart flat and car; flat and car went. She was soon radicalized.

After much encouragement from new friends she made when she was living in squats, she talked herself onto a course at a polytechnic and has for some years been a social worker for the London borough of Lambeth, specializing in the care of the elderly.

She is a favourite with her clients, who call her Blondie, but she doesn't have much time for men under sixty-five years old except for her adored baby son, conceived in a fit of absence of mind after a demonstration in support of the miners' strike in the summer of 1984. She and her baby live in a communal house in Tulse Hill. She stood unsuccessfully as a Labour candidate in the last local elections. She lost to the Alliance but has been promised a safe ward next time.

She knows Rosie Collins from Greenham Common but the name Collins isn't unusual enough to jog her memory and she never has any reason to think of Lee; why should she? Nor the time, as a matter of fact.

Carolyn . . . is now a TV presenter with one of the commercial channels. After her first marriage, to a television journalist, came unstuck, she married a young barrister who was just beginning to make a name for himself; he has now done so. They have a house in Kentish Town, cottages in Suffolk and the Dordogne, and a full-time nanny for their daughter, Emma. Carolyn's son by her first marriage, Gareth, is at boarding school. She recently joined the SDP.

At first I thought there could be no positive future for *Buzz* but prison, either for dealing or for committing grievous bodily harm. That is because the essence of naturalist fiction is plausibility; in order to create the willing suspension of disbelief, the writer is forced to allot his or her characters lives that are the most plausible, not the most like life, which, since it is not the product of the human imagination, holds infinite surprises. It would be plausible, and morally satisfying, to dispatch Buzz to prison for some years, though God help the other inmates; but real life goes something like this:

In 1969, Buzz was still waiting for his historic moment, which is why he is the least resolved character in the novel. You might have taken him for a wilting floweroid if you had met him then but, in fact, he was simply waiting for punk to happen, and if he could have contrived to get through the next four or five years without death or addiction, he would become rich and famous.

He added a third z (Buzzz) and managed a few early punk bands with some flair but he had always enjoyed throwing parties almost more than anything and found his metier when he imparted the very quality of 'The Masque of the Red Death' that characterized his most successful thrashes to the clubs he managed in London and, from 1977, New York, where he has also dabbled in real estate with some success.

He now lives a life of paranoid seclusion in a midtown penthouse, surrounded by a covey of leather-clad acolytes. His videos are spoken of with bated breath. He was early into graffiti and runs a specialist gallery on the upper East Side, besides the notorious performance-art venue in SoHo and a bondage joint in the East Village. Wim Wenders is rumoured to be considering a treatment based on the search Buzzz undertook for his father in the Apache reservations of the Southwest in early 1980, as a follow-up to *Paris, Texas.*

The brothers are no longer in communication. Their endless, pointless quarrel as to which of them was responsible for finally pushing Annabel over the edge was never resolved, became slurred and desultory on Lee's part and was abandoned when Buzzz moved to London shortly after Lee was taken in hand by the young woman who later married him. Nevertheless, Lee is the only human being his brother ever felt one scrap for and he admits to himself, and occasionally to startled companions, that if there is one thing he would like to do before he dies, it is to fuck him. There is as much menace as desire in this wish.

The portrait by Robert Maplethorpe reproduced in the Sunday colour supplements two or three years ago shows he has not changed, much, except for the ring in his nipple.

Lee was rehabilitated from a slough of guilt, misery, impotence, self-pity and drug and alcohol abuse by a stern and passionate young supply teacher of English, who was at that time a member of the SWP (or IS as it was known then). He still believes it was his first name she found so irresistible; certainly little else about him was attractive at that time.

Rosie fought to reclaim his soul for the revolution and his

body for the use of women with missionary zeal and by the time, around 1972, she reluctantly came to the conclusion that the revolution was not imminent in Britain, their first child was on its way. Her father, a south London newsagent, offered them enough money for the deposit on a small house if they legitimized the grandchild. So their fates were sealed. Lee lives in a street that is the twin of the one in which he grew up; his aunt would have approved of his wife. He vaguely marvels when something – Jimi Hendrix on the radio, perhaps; a glimpse of his former philosophy tutor – reminds him of his hot, glorious, cruel youth.

Lee turned out to be rather a good teacher. He works extremely hard in a huge (2,800) comprehensive school, is active in the union and, at home, does most of the cooking as Rosie is not talented in that direction. He is too tired to be unfaithful, even if the opportunity arose.

When he and Rosie first lived together, they spent much time analysing the catastrophe of Lee's relationship with Annabel. Initially, Rosie thought it must have been a simple tragedy of propinquity – three people who should never have had anything to do with one another forced together by circumstances beyond their control, such as birth and love. She did not want to blame Lee, nor Lee to blame himself. But, as she encountered and absorbed the women's movement, she found she had no option but to do so, blaming him for sins of omission and commission, and, especially, for raising his hand to Annabel, that frail, tragic creature.

By the time of the three-day week, the ghost of Annabel was exerting such pressure on them that Rosie could endure it no longer, scooped up her little girl and left home. Lee endured their absence with unexpected stoicism, keeping up the mortgage repayments, staying away from drink and women; each night he stepped inside the empty room where the torn poster of Minnie Mouse in aviatrix's garb still fluttered forlornly on the wall and stared at the empty cot with such intensity he might have been attempting to teleport its rightful occupant home by sheer force of will.

All the same, it takes a lot to make a man admit he has been a bastard, even a man so prone to masochistic self-abnegation as Lee. And, at the period of his very worst behaviour, he had no idea of how big a bastard he was being. Nowadays he can hardly bear to think his daughters might meet young men like him; he does not know that one of them already has.

Rosie finally resolved her argument with him to her own satisfaction by deciding that, yes, he *was* a hypocrite, but if she were to remain a heterosexual, then she could go farther and fare worse. Besides, the little girl adored her father and made her mother feel dreadful about keeping them apart. So they returned home in the period of muted, and, as it turned out, illusory optimism following the Labour victory in the 1974 elections.

By then, Lee had recovered his looks and spirits. Even now, past forty and running somewhat to fat, he is still a physically glamorous man, or he would have no meaning. Rosie would never own up in public to the pleasure his blond, dishevelled presence gives her because, in their austere circles, it would not be considered a sound basis for a lasting relationship. But it has served its turn where Lee and Rosie are concerned. They quarrel a good deal, but he is always grateful to her, in spite of what he says, for bringing him out of his private chamber of horrors, even if sometimes he resents it; Buzzz has made a small fortune out of the very same chamber of horrors, after all.

A second little girl followed in due course after the family was reunited. (The third, a latecomer, is still in arms.) Lee was astonished by the violence of his passion for his children. Rosie got the job at the Community Centre. Lee moved to another school as deputy head of department. The minutiae of everyday life consumed them.

Why should Lee be rewarded with a stable relationship? Might it not be almost as much a punishment as a reward? What sane person would voluntarily choose a life of hard work, ideological integrity and compulsive domesticity in the English provinces over one of terminal chic in New York City? Rosie's lips go thin and white when their lifelong disagreement takes this turn. *She* would, for one. She remembers how Lee drove his first wife mad and then killed her. She reminds him of this; she and Lee share a rare talent for the unforgivable. She suggests that degeneracy runs in Lee's family. They row fiercely. The adolescent daughters in their attic room turn up the volume of the record player to drown the noise. Upstairs, the baby cries. The telephone rings. Rosie springs off to answer. It is the Women's Refuge. She begins an animated conversation about wife-beating, raising two fingers to her husband in an obscene gesture.

The screaming baby is plentifully extruding a foul-smelling substance similar in colour and consistency to spinach purée. Lee inspects it anxiously, as a Roman soothsayer might have peered at entrails. He cleans her up, muttering to himself about Rosie's shortcomings as a mother in order to obscure his worry, If this keeps up, the baby must go to the clinic first thing in the morning. He paces the room for a while, pressing her hot, miserable weight against his breast, on which there is still a tattooed heart; Rosie has grown so used to it she doesn't notice it any more. Suddenly the whimpering baby yawns hugely, quiets and sleeps, looking all at once like a blessed infant.

Her father kisses her moist, meagre hair and lays her down upon her side. The older girls, trained in deference to her tyrannic sleeps, snap off their loud music but, cold-eyed strangers that they have become, continue to discuss in muted whispers their parents' deficiencies as human beings.

Oh, the pain of it, thought Lee, thinking about his children, oh! the exquisite pain of unrequited love. The only authentic wound, the sweet curse they inflict on you, the revenge of heterosexuality.